Unwanted visitors!

I was fourteen years old, sitting in our one-room country school on a beautiful spring afternoon, and my life seemed to be moving as slowly as an ant.

My eyes had wandered to one of the three windows on the south side of our school and I was staring off at the canyons, and beyond them, the broad valley of the Canadian River. Around Notla School, the land was as flat as a kitchen table, but just a mile to the south the country fell suddenly into those deep canyons. That's where our ranch began, on the edges of those canyons. I had ridden through them on horseback, and on long lazy days in school, I enjoyed looking at them out the window.

But all at once I noticed something odd. Off in the distance, near the head of Point Creek Canyon, I saw what appeared to be a line of pack animals.

I sat up and looked closer. There were five of them. No, six. They were just specks on the horizon, moving slowly in single file. And they were on our ranch.

Moonshiner's GOLD

JOHN R. ERICKSON

PUFFIN BOOKS

PUFFIN BOOKS
Published by the Penguin Group
Penguin Putnam Books for Young Readers,
345 Hudson Street, New York, New York 10014, U.S.A.
Penguin Books Ltd, 80 Strand, London WC2R ORL, England
Penguin Books Australia Ltd,
250 Camberwell Road, Camberwell, Victoria 3124, Australia
Penguin Books Canada Ltd, 10 Alcorn Avenue, Toronto, Ontario, Canada M4V 3B2
Penguin Books (N.Z.) Ltd, 182-190 Wairau Road, Auckland 10, New Zealand

Penguin Books Ltd, Registered Offices: Harmondsworth, Middlesex, England

First published in the United States of America by Viking,
a division of Penguin Putnam Books for Young Readers, 2001
Published by Puffin Books,
a division of Penguin Putnam Books for Young Readers, 2003

1 3 5 7 9 10 8 6 4 2

THE LIBRARY OF CONGRESS HAS CATALOGED THE VIKING EDITION AS FOLLOWS:
Erickson, John R., date
Moonshiner's gold: a novel / by John R. Erickson
p. cm.
Summary: In Canadian, Texas, in 1927, not long after his father's death, Riley
and his fiddle-playing grandfather must find a way to save the family ranch
from a group of moonshiners and the men behind their operation.
ISBN 0-670-03502-5
[1. Grandfather—Fiction. 2. Criminals—Fiction. 3. Prohibition—Fiction.
4. Texas—Fiction.] I. Title.
PZ7.E72556 Mom 2001 [Fic]—dc21   2001017989

Puffin Books ISBN 0-14-250023-2

Printed in the United States of America

For Frankie, my friend and teacher.

And for Kristin Gilson, my editor at Puffin Books,

who labored long and hard on this book.

Chapter One

OCTOBER 1926

OCTOBER 4, 1926, was one of those warm still Indian summer days in the Texas Panhandle. The cottonwoods and willows along the Canadian River had begun to show their autumn colors. You could see forever and hear sounds from miles away.

As we drove into town for the funeral, Aunt Mattie commented on the pretty red and orange leaves on the skunkbrush and wild plum bushes. Mother nodded and smiled. I don't suppose she noticed the fall colors. Or maybe she did and was remembering that fall had been my father's favorite season.

People were gathering at the Presbyterian church

when we arrived, and the hearse was parked out front. Mother walked to the hearse and paused a moment. I thought she might start crying, but she didn't. What I saw in her eyes was grief and fear of the future.

Inside the church, the congregation rose when we, the immediate family, entered: Aunt Mattie and Uncle George Sparrow; Mother; Coy, my little brother; and I. A lady from town was playing hymns on an upright piano which needed tuning, and the minister, a young man who served churches in Canadian and Briscoe, stood at the front, holding a big Bible and an envelope with notes written on the back.

When we had seated ourselves near the front, the congregation sat down. The lady played one hymn after another. The minister scowled and glanced at his pocket watch. Aunt Mattie's eyes prowled the church, and at last she couldn't stand it any longer. She leaned across me and hissed to Mother, *"Where is he?"*

The fiddle player was late for the funeral. The fiddle player was my grandfather, Abner Dawson.

Moving her eyes ever so slightly, Mother told me to go look for him, so I left the church and went running through town, asking if anyone had seen Abner Dawson. It was embarrassing, a thirteen-year-old boy chasing around town to find his grandfather.

At the livery barn, Mr. Dooley offered me his big rough hand. "Riley, we'll miss your daddy. He was a fine man. How are y'all holding up?"

"We'll make it . . . I guess. Have you seen my grandfather?"

"If your mother needs anything, give me a holler." Mr. Dooley frowned. "Abner drove into town about an hour ago. You might check the domino parlor."

The domino parlor was not a place where boys often went. It was a haven for men, most of them old, where they could cuss and laugh, tell stories, smoke nasty cigars, and play dominoes, without irritating their wives and daughters. Another attraction of the domino parlor was that the men could buy and sip moonshine whiskey, which, during Prohibition, was supposed to be illegal.

It was hard to understand Prohibition. If it was illegal to make, sell, and drink liquor, why was it available on Main Street in Canadian, Texas?

When I walked into the domino parlor, the place fell silent, as the men stared at me and wondered why a boy had invaded their sanctuary. The only sound came from a table at the rear, where two men were playing a tune on their fiddles. One was an old farmer in overalls. The other, a smallish elf of a man dressed in a rumpled black suit, high-topped boots, and a dusty cowboy hat, was Abner Dawson.

Bert Rawls, a retired rancher, must have figured out why I was there. He cupped his hand around his mouth and called out, "Abner, what time was that funeral?"

The music stopped. Grampy's head snapped back and I heard him say, "Uh-oh." He threw his fiddle into the case and came running to the door. "Hello, boy. I lost track of the time."

I stared at him. "How could you be late for my father's funeral?"

His blue eyes turned sad. "I'm sorry, son, I truly am."

That was Grampy Dawson: late, irresponsible, and truly sorry.

We ran up the hill toward the courthouse, until Grampy was gasping for breath and had to slow to a walk. He pulled a blue bandana out of his hip pocket and mopped his face. "What happened to Jim?"

"Nobody's sure. He was riding a good gentle horse in Picket Canyon and he didn't come in for lunch. Spud Morris found him. Maybe the horse spooked and bucked him off."

Grampy frowned and stuffed the bandana back into his pocket. "How's your momma doing?"

"Well, she's a widow with two boys and a ranch to run. I'd guess she's scared."

"Son, I'm sure sorry about your daddy. I liked Jim. He was a fine man."

"Thanks. We expected you last night."

"I came as soon as I got the news, drove all night."

"Where were you this time?"

"Down near Childress. I've been trading a few horses and playing them old dances."

"Will you stay a while this time?"

"Uh . . . we'll have to see about that." By the time we made it to the church steps, Grampy had to stop and catch his breath again. "Did my sister come?" I nodded. Yes, Aunt Mattie was waiting inside the church, she and a lot of other people. Grampy winced. "I'm sure I'll hear about this for a long time."

We entered the church. Grampy removed his hat and tried to tiptoe down the aisle, but the floorboards squeaked on every step, and everyone heard us coming. Aunt Mattie beamed Grampy a cold blue-eyed glare all the way down the aisle.

The funeral service was a disappointment to me. Reverend Morrison hadn't lived in the community for very long and didn't know my father well. And he didn't have much understanding of ranch people. There were many things he could have said but didn't: Jim McDaniels was an honest man, a horseman, a judge of good cattle, and a pretty salty roper; he always paid his debts and kept up his fences.

Reverend Morrison did his best, I suppose. The service would have been all right for some men, but it didn't do justice to my father.

Later, at the cemetery, Reverend Morrison said a few words, and then Grampy got up and played "Amazing Grace" on his fiddle. Before he started playing, I could see judgment in the eyes of some of the townspeople. They probably thought that a barndance musician had no place at a Christian funeral, that Abner Dawson belonged in a saloon, not at a funeral service.

That thought had even occurred to me.

But then Grampy rested the fiddle under his chin, closed his eyes, and moved the bow across the strings. The first notes of "Amazing Grace" floated out into the soft autumn air—a deep, eerie sound that sent chills down the back of my neck. I'd never heard Grampy Dawson play a hymn before, and wouldn't have bet that he even knew one. But he did. Somehow and from somewhere, he pulled notes out of the fiddle that expressed my feelings of grief and loss.

Others in the crowd must have been touched too. Mother's eyes were shining. The young minister seemed to be in a trance. Three grave diggers, rough laboring men leaning on their shovels, listened to every note. Even Aunt Mattie seemed moved, though I'm sure she didn't want anyone to know it.

When Grampy let the last note of the song fade away, I stared at him in wonder. I had never understood this man. He had been in and out of my life for as long as I could remember, but he never stayed around long enough for me to get to know him.

When Grampy finished and was putting away his fiddle, the minister walked over to him. "Mr. Dawson, I've heard a lot about you."

Grampy looked over his shoulder at the young man and said, "Uh-oh."

"And it was all true. Sir, that was beautiful! 'Amazing Grace' has never been done better."

Aunt Mattie eased up to Grampy. With her arms folded across her chest, she looked like a coiled snake. "Abner, I can't deny that you played that thing mighty pretty, but one hymn at a funeral don't make up for the life of a gypsy. And," she leaned forward and whispered in his ear, "you've got whiskey on your breath!"

"Why, Mattie, surely not. We're in Prohibition, you know."

"Prohibition, my foot! That law's got more holes in it than Swiss cheese."

Mother came up and stepped between them. She and Grampy looked into each other's eyes for a long moment. Neither knew what to say. Then Mother pulled him into an embrace. "Daddy, I'm so glad you came. Your music was wonderful. Jim would have loved it."

Grampy smiled. "Sugar, I'm so sorry about Jim. What will you do now?"

"I guess we'll stay on the ranch. I don't know where else to go."

"You know, Sara, I've been thinking . . ."

Mother put a finger to his lips. "Shhh. Don't say it, Daddy. Don't make promises you can't keep."

It appeared that Grampy wanted to say more, but he didn't.

After the funeral, we drove back to the ranch. Coy and I rode in the car with Aunt Mattie and Uncle George, while Mother rode with Grampy in his old Model T Ford truck.

Aunt Mattie was actually my great-aunt, Grampy Dawson's sister, and she and Uncle George had been married only a couple of years. They lived in the town of Sparrow, some seventy miles up the Canadian River from our ranch. Uncle George had been one of the founders of the town, and it had been named after him. He was a tall, silent man in his seventies, whose face reminded me of wax or alabaster.

Coy and I had heard whispers that Uncle George was as rich as Midas.

Among Uncle George's many real estate holdings was the ranch we lived on. We leased it and ran 250 mother cows on 6,000 acres of rough canyon country. There were better cow ranches in Hemphill County, but Daddy had always loved the place and had admired its rugged beauty. And so far, we'd been able to make a living on it.

It was odd that Mattie Dawson, an old maid into her fifties, had married into the name Sparrow, because she had qualities that reminded me of a bird. She was a tiny woman, no more than five feet tall, with restless blue eyes and the rapid metabolism of a starling or a sparrow.

As we bounced and lurched down the dirt road that ran parallel to the Canadian River, Aunt Mattie sat in the front, darting looks at the big empty ranch country beyond her window and muttering under her breath. Uncle George drove and said nothing.

"Abner drives too fast. Always has. It's a fine thing, him showing up late to Jim's funeral! George, I don't understand why Ben Wallace insisted you buy this godforsaken ranch. I don't see how Sara can stand to live out here." She coughed and covered her nose with a white hankie. "This dust will kill us all! George, you haven't said two words all day."

He gave her a blank look. "We're a good match."

Just then, we looked up and saw a car approaching from the west. Uncle George jerked the wheel and managed to avoid a head-on collision. As the car passed, I caught a glimpse of two men, both dressed in dark suits and hats.

Aunt Mattie frowned. "Why, that looked like Ben Wallace. What would a doctor be doing out here in the middle of nowhere?"

Uncle George said, "Seems odd, don't it?" There was a long silence. "You know, I think he's gone crooked."

Aunt Mattie's eyes narrowed. "Ben? He's your business partner. He's also the nicest, politest man I know."

Uncle George shrugged and said no more.

Aunt Mattie and Uncle George stayed at the ranch for an hour, then went back home to Sparrow. Around sundown, Grampy Dawson spread out his bedroll in our little barn. I asked if he would rather sleep on the back porch, but he said no. When he came to visit, he never stayed in the house. He said it was too small, and besides, he'd gotten used to sleeping in his old cowboy bedroll. That was his home, he said.

I had thought Grampy might stay around for a while, to help us adjust to living without Daddy. But the next morning at daylight, I looked out the window and saw that his truck was gone. He left us a note scrawled in pencil on a scrap of lumber.

"Dear Ones: Have business to take care of, 2

dances and a pen of bronc horses. Will return when possible. Stay well. Abner S. Dawson."

Six months later, in April of 1927, we got word that George Sparrow had died in his sleep. We had no telephone on the ranch and word didn't reach us until after the funeral. His heart gave out, they said, and there was no suffering. He was seventy-eight years old.

Overnight, Aunt Mattie became the richest woman in the Texas Panhandle.

Chapter Two

MAY 14, 1927

SOMEWHERE IN THE back of my mind, I could hear Miss Cates's voice. She was telling the class about Hannibal's march over the Alps. They were riding on . . . was it elephants or camels? Some strange animal.

I was fourteen years old, sitting in our one-room country school on a beautiful spring afternoon, and my life seemed to be moving as slowly as an ant.

My eyes had wandered to one of the three windows on the south side of our school and I was staring off at the canyons, and beyond them, the broad valley of the Canadian River. Around Notla School, the land was as flat as a kitchen table, but just a mile to the south the country fell suddenly into those deep canyons. That's where our ranch began, on the edges of those canyons. I had ridden through most of them on horseback, and on long lazy days in school, I enjoyed looking at them out the window.

But all at once I noticed something odd. Off in the distance, near the head of Point Creek Canyon, I saw what appeared to be a line of pack animals.

I sat up and looked closer. There were five of them. No, six. They were just specks on the horizon, moving slowly in single file. And they were on *our ranch*.

"Riley, what was the purpose of Hannibal's march over the Alps? Riley? Riley McDaniels!"

I tore my gaze away from the window and turned it toward the woman in the black speckled dress, Miss Cates. Since midterm she had been our teacher. She was tall and skinny, and had a small mouth. She wore her hair pulled up in a bun and she had a mole on her left cheek.

And there she stood at the front of the room, stiff and earnest, holding a big history book in her hands, and glaring at me over the tops of her glasses.

"Riley? Are you listening to the lesson or daydreaming?"

"Listening, Miss Cates."

"Good. Why was Hannibal crossing the Alps on an elephant?"

"I'm not sure, ma'am."

Coy's arm shot up like a little skyrocket. He was

sitting at the front, where Miss Cates's pets always sat, and he knew the answer.

Coy *always* knew the answers to her questions. He was the most obnoxious little twerp in our whole school of thirty-five kids. He was in sixth grade, two grades below me. He was a small kid for his age, had a rooster tail at the back of his head, and wore big glasses that made him look like an owl.

To look at Coy, you never would have guessed that he was a ranch kid. You'd have thought he was born in a library. He'd never cared much about horses or dogs or the important things in life, and he hated dirt. It was sad to see a ranch kid who had been so corrupted by books, who'd turned out to be such an annoying little do-right.

Coy was exactly the kind of kid I'd always hoped to avoid and never speak to. Unfortunately, I couldn't avoid him and I had to speak to him every once in a while.

He was my little brother.

School finally ended that afternoon at three o'clock. As soon as I stepped out into the school yard, I could see that Coy had already gotten himself into an argument with Jackie Tinsley. Unless I intervened, Coy would get thrashed. Coy deserved most of his thrashings, but this time there was a higher principle involved: Coy was a McDaniels, and Jackie was a Tinsley.

Jackie's father was one of the biggest landowners in

our part of the world. Their ranch, which joined ours on the east, covered something like 50,000 acres, making it eight times bigger than our place. Jackie had his ways of reminding us that we were quite a bit beneath the Tinsley standards. He sometimes called us "sharecroppers," because we rented our land.

So I made a detour, seized my little brother by the arm, and pulled him away. Since I was fourteen years old, I had to bring some maturity to these schoolyard arguments.

Coy was red-faced and fuming. "He can't say that!"

"What did he say?"

"He said . . . he said that Grampy Dawson warms his false teeth in his coffee every morning!"

"Coy, he does. We laugh about that all the time."

"Well, *we* can laugh but *he* can't. He's making fun."

"Come on, or it'll be dark before we get home."

"And then he said that Grampy's a shiftless, ne'er-do-well musician!"

"Coy, sticks and stones may break your bones, but words will never . . . he said *that?*"

"He sure did!"

I turned on my heel and marched over to Jackie, who was now laughing with some other boys. "Jackie, what did you just say about my grandfather?"

Jackie's eyes came up. He noticed, I'm sure, that I had grown three inches since school started in September, and had added some hard muscle to my bones. Jackie had always been able to take me down in a scuffle, and had made me eat dirt on several occasions. But we hadn't squared off in six months, and now he wasn't so sure how it might end up.

He looked me over. "I said . . . he's a pretty good fiddle player."

"Oh. Well, you're right about that. Thanks. See you boys Monday."

Coy felt compelled to fire one last shot at Jackie Tinsley. "And for your stupid information, Grampy Dawson used to be sheriff of Dodge City!"

Jackie was already out of hearing range, so Coy was safe. We made our way to the hitching rail, where Laura Higgins was waiting with the horses. I rode a little gray Arabian mare named Dolly. Laura was mounted on her bay mare, Ruthie, and Coy rode old Socks. We tightened the cinches on our saddles and started the long ride home.

Laura's family farmed up on the flats about three miles west of the school, and Coy and I always rode the first two miles with her before we turned and headed south off the caprock and into the canyons. In doing this, I risked being teased by the other boys who always tried to find romance in any friendship between a boy and a girl, but Laura was worth the risk.

We were friends, that was all, and she couldn't help it that she was a girl. Laura had no more use for romance than I did. You could talk about things with Laura. She liked dogs, wasn't scared of snakes, and could ride a horse as well as anyone.

As we rode along, I cut a glance at my brother. His lower lip was sticking out and he still looked mad.

"Coy, if you don't pull in that lip, your horse is going to step on it."

"When I grow up, I'm going to beat up Jackie Tinsley every day."

"By the time you grow up, Jackie will be an old man on a crutch. In the meantime, I'd be grateful if you'd quit drawing me into your battles."

"I didn't ask for your help."

"I did it for the good name of our ranch. If you're going to be a worm, learn to be humble."

"I'm not a worm."

"You *are* a worm. You're a bookworm, and one of these days I'm going to stop getting involved in your problems."

With that out of the way, Laura and I rode together, while Coy pulled out his book and started reading about knights and damsels. He was able to read on horseback because Socks was as gentle as a pup and would follow my horse anywhere.

For a long time, Laura and I said nothing. I liked that about her. She didn't chatter. She could enjoy the smells of spring, the wildflowers, the beauty of the country, and she didn't need to talk about it.

After a while, she said, "Is that true? Was your grandfather sheriff of Dodge City?"

"No, that's Coy's version. Grampy worked as a brand inspector for the Cattle Raisers for a while, and before that, he was a cowboy on the Matador Ranch. Coy has an active imagination."

"Have you heard from him?"

"Grampy?" I looked away. "Not since the funeral. I guess he'll show up when his socks need darning."

Laura let the subject drop. She understood about Grampy Dawson. Mother needed his help, but as usual, he had other fish to fry.

I glanced over my shoulder, to be sure that Coy wasn't eavesdropping. "Laura, you know when the teacher called on me and I couldn't answer the question? I was looking out the window, and I saw the strangest thing—a pack train going into Point Creek Canyon."

"On your ranch? Who was it?"

"I don't know, but I'd sure like to find out."

By then, we had come to the place where Coy and I turned south. I got down and opened the gate for Laura. "Well, see you Monday—the last day of school! I can hardly wait."

Laura nodded and smiled. "Riley, you weren't thinking of riding into that canyon, were you?"

"That spooky place? Heck no."

"Daddy has told us *never* to go into the canyons."

"I wonder why."

"He didn't say."

Laura waved good-bye and rode on to the west. I found my eyes following her and watching as the wind teased her long red hair.

Chapter Three

WHEN COY AND I left Laura, we turned our horses and rode on. Or to be more accurate, I turned my horse and Coy's horse followed. Coy still had his nose in the book and didn't notice that I was heading southeast, toward Point Creek Canyon. Usually, we rode straight south, along the rim of Picket Canyon.

For fifteen minutes we rode in silence. That was fine with me. I had nothing to say to Coy and he certainly had nothing that I wanted to hear.

Then he spoke up. "I wonder how those knights walked in their suits of armor."

"What?"

"Those knights in the old days, they wore all that heavy armor. How do you reckon they walked?"

"Well, they didn't walk, Coy. They rode. They were horsemen. That's what made them so noble. A man on a horse is always more noble than a man who walks."

"But how did they get into the saddle?"

"They climbed up into a tree and jumped down."

He thought about that for a moment. "They did not. Riley, climbing a tree in a steel suit would be even harder than mounting a horse."

"In that case, I don't know. Now put your book away and look at the country. Use your eyes, before you blind yourself reading."

He put the book into his saddlebag, glanced around and blinked his eyes. "Hey, this isn't the way home."

We had come to the rim of the canyon. "We're taking a different route. You need some adventure, O Little One."

"Stop calling me that. I hate it. And I'm not going into that canyon. Mother wouldn't approve, you know that."

I started down the rugged trail that led into the canyon. It had been carved out of the limestone rock by the hooves of countless mule deer, but it had also been used that very afternoon by a man leading pack animals. I saw their tracks, and showed them to Coy.

Coy whined and protested, but he followed me down the trail. I knew he would—because he was scared to ride home by himself.

It was a rough and spooky place, that canyon. The canyon walls rose straight up and the cedar forest was so thick, nothing grew on the ground and you could hardly ride a horse through it without getting your clothes torn off.

Coy and I had explored some of the canyons on our ranch, but there were several places we'd never dared to go. Point Creek Canyon was one of them. It was so far away from anything, so quiet and isolated . . . if anything happened to you in that canyon, if your horse fell or bucked you off, nobody would find you for hours or days.

That's what had happened to our father.

We made it to the bottom and followed the tracks toward the cedar forest that grew around a spring. All at once I caught the smell of smoke. Cedar smoke. It has a very distinctive smell.

Coy smelled it too, and it scared him. "Riley, I don't like this. Let's go home."

I told him to calm down. Somebody had built a campfire in our canyon, and I wanted to find out who and why.

We rode as far as we could ride, until the cedar branches became so thick that they were clawing at our clothes. We dismounted and crawled through the trees. The smell of smoke was getting heavier as we went. At last we reached a spot where we could see the campfire. But that wasn't all we saw.

This wasn't just a place where a man had stopped to boil some coffee. It appeared that somebody had been *camped for days.* We saw bedding, cooking pots, cans of food, a shovel, an ax, a pile of wood, a coil of rope, a coal oil lantern, even a cane-bottom chair.

Somebody was *living in our canyon.*

Once we got over that shock, there was another one waiting for us. Beside the spring pool stood five or six wooden hogshead barrels, a stack of hundred-pound burlap sacks, and a big copper pot with a long coil of copper tubing.

Coy looked at me and I looked at him.

Coy's lips formed one word: "Moonshiners?" I nodded.

We'd never met a moonshiner, but we'd heard stories whispered around school. They were gangsters, outlaws, bad men who made whiskey, and everyone's advice on moonshiners was . . . *stay away from them!*

That's why Laura's daddy had told her never to go into the canyons.

I shot a glance at Coy and saw that his face was as pale as oatmeal. Maybe mine was too. I was about to give Coy the sign to move out when my ears picked up a new sound.

Click. Click.

Coy heard it too. His eyes grew wide with fear and I could see that his lower lip had begun to tremble. There was no mistaking what we'd heard. It was the crisp click of double-barrel shotgun hammers.

With a feeling of dread, I turned my eyes toward the sound, and sure enough, there was a pair of old black boots showing beneath the undergrowth. Someone was standing beside our horses. And I heard a man's voice.

"I reckon you might as well come out of there. Keep your hands up high and don't make any sudden moves."

Behind me, Coy whispered, "Riley?" He was scared.

"Hush, Coy. Be brave and do as he says."

We raised our hands as high as we could and stepped out into the little clearing where we had left the horses. And that's when we got our first look at a real live moonshiner.

He was a tall man, lean and muscular, with coal-black eyes and long dirty hair hanging below an old fedora hat. A hand-rolled cigarette dangled from one side of his mouth and he held the shotgun at his waist.

The holes in that shotgun barrel looked as big as cannonballs.

When we stepped out of the cedar and he got a look at us, a smile twitched at one corner of his mouth. "Well, lawsy me. It's a couple of kids." The smile disappeared. "You boys alone? Don't lie."

I tried to answer, but my voice had turned to a croak. I cleared my throat and tried again. "Yes sir, we're alone. I'm Riley McDaniels, and this is my brother Coy. We're riding home from school."

He barked a little laugh. "School, huh? Well now, you've found yourself a whole new kind of school here, haven't you?" Then he turned his head to the right and yelled, "Red! It's a couple of kids."

Red came out of the cedars, a stout man dressed in greasy blue overalls. He wore no shirt, and his arms and shoulders were covered with thick red hair. "What are you gonna do with 'em, Charlie?"

"Don't know yet. I'm studying on it." Charlie turned back to us. "Red, he don't like people much." Charlie narrowed his eyes and looked us up and down. "You boys know what we're doing here?"

"Moonshine?"

He nodded. "That's it. Canyon rum, Prohibition gold."

"Sir, we didn't know . . . we were just on our way home from school and we smelled smoke. This is our ranch and we wanted to see what was going on."

Charlie squinted against the smoke of the cigarette. I had a feeling that he was still trying to decide what to do with us. "Does your momma know where you're at?"

"No sir, I . . . I don't think so."

He grinned, showing brown-stained teeth. "I'll bet she don't. If she did, she'd whale you both with a big old stick." He dropped his cigarette to the ground and stepped on it. "Most usually, when we have visitors, we cut off their ears. Red, fetch me that big butcher knife."

Coy gasped and stared at me with huge eyes. Red laughed and went back into the trees. Charlie watched him, then turned to me and whispered, "Just teasing. Quick, y'all get out of here and don't come back! Go!"

Coy and I were too scared and shocked to ask any

23

questions. We ran to our horses, leaped up into the saddles, and rode away as fast as we could go. Behind us, I heard Red shout, "Hey! How come you let 'em go? The constable won't like that, Charlie."

And Charlie said, "He don't need to know, Red."

The constable? Is that what he'd said? I didn't have time to think about it.

Off we went like a streak of wind, with poor little Coy halfway on and halfway off, draped over Socks's neck and holding on for dear life. I figured he'd find some way of staying on, and sure enough, he did. He wasn't *about* to fall off that horse.

One of our father's hard and fast rules about horses was "never run a horse toward the barn." It was a good rule and I understood the reason for it. Once you let a horse run toward home, he'll want to do it every time, and before you know it, you'll have yourself a barn-spoiled horse that can't be stopped, no matter how hard you pull on the bits.

But this was a special occasion, and we broke the rule into a thousand pieces. We ran our horses as fast as we dared, the whole two miles back to the house. Coy was yelling at me to slow down, but I didn't. We didn't slow down until we reached the house.

Turk, our dog, heard us coming and came out to bark. When he saw who we were, he ran beside us. Mother and Spud Morris, our hired man, had just returned from feeding cattle in the wagon. Mother was wearing her polka-dot sunbonnet to protect her face from the sun. She was stepping down from the wagon when she saw us coming in.

"Riley, you boys had better quit racing those horses!" But then she saw the looks on our faces and had figured out that something was wrong. Mothers know.

I hadn't intended to tell her about the moonshiners. I didn't want her to worry about it, but I told her the whole story. I knew she'd find out eventually. I'd never been very good at keeping secrets from her.

Our supper that night was a quiet affair. Mother hardly said a word and she picked at her food. Spud must have sensed that something was wrong, and when he'd finished eating, he excused himself and went out to his little cabin. That left us alone.

Mother heaved a deep sigh. "Boys, I thought we were safe out here, away from all the rot of this whiskey business. But here they are, right on the ranch!"

I nodded. "But why *here*, Mother? We're thirty miles from the nearest town."

"Maybe that's the point. I don't know. Tomorrow morning, Spud and I had better take the wagon into Canadian and talk to the sheriff."

Coy looked up from his plate. "I wish Grampy were here. He'd know what to do."

I stared at my brother. "Oh, sure he would."

Chapter Four

AT TEN O'CLOCK Mother kissed us good night and went into her room. Coy made up his bed on the sofa, and I went out to the screen porch. That's where Turk and I slept.

I fell right off to sleep, thinking of our adventure in Point Creek Canyon. The next thing I knew, Turk was barking, and it was his *serious* bark, not his answer-the-coyotes bark. I sat up and looked around. It was as dark as the inside of a cow, but then . . .

There was the flash of light on the wall. I looked off to the south and saw a pair of headlights. They were coming toward the house. A chill moved down my backbone.

I leaped out of my bedroll, felt around on the floor for my pants, and started yelling. "Mother, wake up! Get the gun, the moonshiners are coming! Hurry!"

I left the screened porch and ran inside the house. I heard Mother's footsteps. She struck a match and lit a stub of a candle. She was wearing a housecoat and she had let her hair down for the night. She looked frightened, and I'm sure I did too. We lived so far out in the country, nobody ever came to our place at night. And when someone did, it usually meant trouble.

Mother found the shotgun and a handful of shells. "Well," she said in a brave voice, "what will be will be."

She blew out the candle. We stood in the dark house and waited. We could hear the hum of a motor and the squeaking of springs. The beam of the lights cut across the trees in front of the house. I had brought Turk inside. He would have gladly gone out to battle, but I didn't want to risk his being shot. Anyone sneaky enough to drive up to a house at night might be mean enough to shoot my dog.

I hoped that Coy would stay asleep. There wasn't anything good or constructive he could contribute, but wouldn't you know it? At the very time when Mother and I needed to focus all our attention on the crisis outside, here he came.

"Mother? Riley? What's all the noise?"

I grabbed him and covered his mouth with my hand. "Hush! Someone's outside. I think it's those moonshiners." He was so shocked, he actually hushed.

Turk growled and bristled. Mother dropped two

shells into the shotgun and snapped it shut. If she was afraid, she didn't show it. We listened and watched and waited. Then, through the stillness of the night, we heard something. It was an odd, high-pitched sound. Was it a squeak? No, more like . . . music.

Someone was playing a fiddle!

Mother heaved a deep sigh and sagged against the door frame. "Merciful heavens. It's Daddy! I don't know whether to shoot him or hug him."

I pulled on my shirt and hurried outside with a lantern. Sure enough, I saw Grampy and another man next to Grampy's old Model T Ford truck.

There he stood, Abner Dawson: his faded jeans tucked into the tops of his boots, his sculpted cowboy hat sitting on his silver head like a crown, a big pearly smile on his mouth, his blue eyes sparkling like a fortune in diamonds, and his old fiddle in his hand.

Coy let out a yell and flew into Grampy's arms. Mother was right behind him. She came running down the steps in her housecoat and threw herself around Grampy's neck. I didn't hug Grampy, but shook his hand. To be honest, I wasn't sure how I felt about his coming back. Just about the time you got comfortable having him around, he'd leave.

But Mother was overjoyed. "Daddy, you old scamp, you just about scared us to death! But, my goodness, I'm glad you're back!"

He laughed and said, "I want y'all to meet my friend. He's a fine young fiddle player from Lakeview, Texas. Jim Bob Wills."

Mother gave Mr. Wills a nod. "Welcome, Mr. Wills. Daddy, why didn't you write and tell us where you were? What if we'd needed you for something?"

Grampy shrugged. "I guess it just slipped my mind, sugar. I've been pretty busy with one thing and another."

After an uncomfortable silence, Mother said, "Well, let's go into the house."

We went into the house and Mother made coffee for the men. We sat around the dinner table and listened as Grampy told us about the dances he and Mr. Wills had played up in Kansas.

Mother was smiling. "Daddy, I'm so glad you're here. You can't imagine!"

Grampy wasn't listening. "Sugar, Jim Bob's got a contract to do a radio show on WBAP in Fort Worth. That's where we're headed, to Fort Worth."

Mother's face crumbled. Grampy didn't notice that he'd just stomped on her hopes.

His eyes were sparkling. "You know, I've always dreamed of playing my fiddle on the radio, and Jim Bob's asked me to . . ."

"Oh. How nice." She couldn't hide the disappointment in her voice.

Grampy was puzzled. "I thought you'd be happy. This is a chance of a lifetime."

"I'm happy for you, Daddy. I guess it's what you've always wanted."

She rose from her chair, went into her room, and closed the door. A moment later, we heard a crash of something breaking, then Mother muttering to herself in an angry tone of voice.

Mr. Wills glanced around the table, pushed his chair back, and slipped out of the house. In the deadly silence, Grampy said, "Boys, all at once I notice a chill in the air. Did I do something wrong?"

I didn't even look at him. There was nothing to say. He rose from the table and tapped on Mother's door.

"Sugar?" No answer. He tapped again. "Sara Helen, I can't talk through this door."

"Go away! Why did you even bother to come back? We were getting along just fine without you."

Grampy scratched the back of his head and scowled. "Maybe we ought to talk about this. Why don't you come out?"

The door flew open, causing Grampy to jump back. There stood his daughter, her eyes burning with anger. "All right, Abner Dawson, if you're man enough to listen, I'll talk!"

Grampy swallowed hard and went inside. The door slammed shut. Coy and I listened as Mother ripped into him.

"You selfish, conceited old coot! You think you can stay gone for months and then come skipping in here with a friend and everything will be sugar and spice? Did it ever occur to you that we might *need you* here? I lost my husband six months ago, and those boys lost their daddy. We've been out here on this ranch, trying to survive while you've been off trading horses and playing your fiddle!"

"Well, sugar . . ."

"I'm worn to a frazzle. Look at these hands! They feel like corncobs. Coy cries for his daddy at night, and now we've got gangsters on this ranch!"

"Gangsters? What are you talking about?"

"Moonshiners! They're in one of the canyons, and this afternoon they threatened your grandsons!"

"Why, sugar, I had no idea . . ." The door opened and Grampy backed out.

Mother's voice followed him. "You'd better go, Daddy. We'll be fine. I'm sorry if I was rude and disrespectful. Now please . . . just leave!"

She slammed the door in his face. Grampy stood there for a moment, so shocked he didn't know what to say or do. Then he walked through the house and was gone. He didn't look at me and Coy, or bother to say good-bye.

Outside, the truck door slammed, the motor started, and the truck drove off into the night.

I heard Mother crying. It made tears come to my eyes, and I got up and went into her room. She had fallen across the bed and was crying into a pillow—I guess to keep us boys from hearing.

I sat down on the edge of the bed and stroked her back. She sat up and we hugged each other.

"I ran him off, Riley. We need him here, but I ran him off! I couldn't help it. Sometimes he makes me so mad . . ."

"You did the right thing, Mother. Don't worry, we'll be all right."

She nodded and wiped her face with a hankie. "Well, at least we know where we stand now. Sometimes it's better . . ."

She didn't finish her sentence. Her eyes had gone to the door. I turned and saw Grampy standing there, his hat in his hands. Tears shimmered in the corners of his eyes.

"Sara, you're right. I've been a sorry excuse for a daddy. I sent Jim Bob on to town to catch the train. I'd like to stay around a few days and help you out . . . if you'll have me."

Mother was speechless. She sat on the edge of the bed for a moment, thinking. "Daddy, you know I hate to ask you favors, but this time we really need you."

"I understand. Tomorrow morning, I'll ride over to the canyon and talk with those moonshiners. Maybe we can get it straightened out."

Before I knew it, I said, "I could go with you. We don't have school."

Grampy's eyes swung around to me. "Better not, son. It ain't a job for a boy."

"I'm not a boy anymore."

"No."

"Please?"

"No, son."

The next morning, Grampy saddled a horse and rode away from the house just after daylight. He didn't know that I was watching, or that I planned to follow him.

Chapter Five

THE SUN WAS just coming up when I rode out of the canyon. I looked off to the east and saw no sign of Grampy. He must have trotted his horse and gotten quite a ways ahead of me, yet when I glanced down at the trail, I didn't see his tracks.

I kicked Dolly into a little jog-trot and pointed her in a northeasterly direction, which would take us to Point Creek Canyon.

But all at once I heard something behind me. I twisted around in the saddle and saw Grampy. He clucked to his horse and trotted up beside me. I noticed that he had his fiddle case tied on behind the cantle of his saddle.

He gave me a hard look. "Son, I thought I said you couldn't come."

"I must have misunderstood."

"Uh-huh. Well, you wasted a trip up the caprock. Run along home."

He rode off to the northeast. I followed him, and after a while, he stopped. "You're a stubborn little whelp, aren't you?"

"I get it from my mother's side of the family."

That brought a little smile. "There's truth in that. All right. Let's go." We headed off across the flats in a trot. After a long silence, Grampy said, "Oh by the way, if you're going to follow somebody, it wouldn't hurt to look down at the ground every once in a while. This horse of mine leaves something called . . . *tracks*."

"I did look for tracks, but I thought I knew what you were going to do."

He snorted. "Son, you can't get up early enough in the morning to figure out what I'm going to do. Even my shadow don't know, and sometimes I lose it and have to go looking for it."

"What *are* you going to do?"

"I'm going to get acquainted with your friends in the canyon, and maybe learn a thing or two."

"Why'd you bring your fiddle?"

"Well, I'm going to try something."

"You mean . . . you're going to play the fiddle for them?"

He nodded and smiled. "They say the fiddle player is always the last to be shot."

I stared at him in amazement.

We rode across the flat country for a mile or so. As we approached the rim of Point Creek Canyon, Grampy started watching the ground, until he found a cow trail leading to the caprock. We stopped there, and he pointed to a windmill down in the canyon.

"I'll set up shop at that windmill. You said that Charlie feller seemed kind of friendly?"

"Yes sir, quite a bit more than Red."

Grampy nodded. "I'll talk to him. You stay up here. If things get out of hand, you whip and spur back to the house, hear?"

Grampy mounted his horse and rode down the trail. Once on the canyon floor, he tied his horse to a cedar tree, brought out his fiddle, and sat down on the edge of the cement stock tank. Up on the canyon rim, I lay down flat and watched. Grampy looked about the size of a grasshopper.

He threw one leg over his other knee, brought up his bow, and started playing. It was a tune I had heard him play many times before, a lively jig called "Taters in the Sandy Land," and he played it as well as ever, only this time he was playing it in a canyon that did something unusual to the sound. It caused it to echo or vibrate, and made it seem louder than normal.

It was eerie, like something out of a dream. Here was this little old man, who seemed no bigger than a clothespin in the depths of the canyon, sitting on a water tank and playing his fiddle. In the still air, the sound was as clear and sharp as the ringing of a bell.

When he finished that tune, he paused to wipe some sweat off his forehead. He went right into another tune, and another. I fetched a small pair of binoculars that I always carried in my saddlebags, sat down on the canyon rim, and searched for any sign of color or movement, but there was nothing. The minutes crawled by.

Then . . . there it was, a flicker of something moving in the cedars. I focused on the spot and saw it again, and slowly the shape of a man emerged. He was creeping through the cedar, and he was carrying a gun, either a shotgun or a rifle.

And then I caught a glimpse of a second man. He was bent over and creeping along the edge of the forest, and he too was carrying a gun. It was Red. I recognized his blue overalls and thick red beard. Then a third man stepped out, and all at once I felt prickles of fear on the back of my neck.

The third man wasn't Charlie, but a large man wearing a black suit and a bowler hat—a very odd kind of dress for a man to wear in such a place. *Where was Charlie?* I felt an impulse to yell a warning, but I didn't dare.

The men emerged from the trees and stood in the clearing, maybe twenty yards north of the windmill. There they stood, guns at the ready, staring at this man playing the fiddle. Grampy went right on playing, just as he did when he was practicing alone. The men exchanged glances and signs. Through the glasses, I could see that they were having a hard time figuring this out.

They didn't know what to do. And sure enough, they didn't shoot the fiddle player.

Then Grampy stopped playing. He turned around and saw the men. He laid his fiddle in the open case and tried to light a little cigar, but his hands were trembling so badly, he finally threw it into the tank.

The big man clapped his hands three times, in a kind of mockery of applause, and walked forward. He reached into his coat pocket and pulled out . . . a peanut, a peanut in the shell. He cracked it open and popped it into his mouth. When he spoke, I could hear every word he said. I guess the canyon walls amplified the sound.

"Do you play here all the time or is this something special?"

Grampy said, "Yesterday afternoon, my grandsons met a man named Charlie. I'd like to speak to him."

The big man glanced at his comrades, and they all laughed. "Well sir, Charlie ain't with us any longer, so maybe you'll have to speak to me. What's on your mind?"

"Hoss, I'll get right to the point. You boys are trespassing on private property. This ranch belongs to my sister, and I don't think she gave you permission to be here."

That brought another round of laughter from the men. "Well, I guess you need to talk to your sister. What else?"

Grampy hitched up his jeans. He seemed to be getting bolder now. "Whose deal is this?"

The big man tossed some nuts into his mouth. "Mister, that kind of information could get a man into trouble. In fact, being here can get a man into trouble. If I was you, I'd climb back on that horse and ride out of here. Fast."

Red moved toward the big man and said, "Hey Joe . . ." He whispered something, and they both laughed.

Then Joe, the big man, turned back to Grampy. "Good idea, Red. We changed the plan, Mr. Fiddle Player. Get on your horse *backward* and ride out of here. Fast."

"I'd rather not do that," said Grampy. Joe lifted the fiddle out of its case and indicated that he might smash it against a leg of the windmill tower. Grampy said, "Or maybe I will."

Red and his pal threw Grampy into the saddle backward, tied his hands behind his back, and tied his feet into the stirrups. Joe watched with a smile and popped peanuts into his mouth.

"There!" said Joe when they were done. "And don't forget your fiddle." He tied the fiddle case onto the saddle with saddle strings. "That was mighty pretty music you played and it's too bad you have to leave so soon. Now, git and don't come back!"

He slapped Grampy's horse on the behind, and Snips ran south down the canyon, followed by the loud echoing laughter of the men. Grampy rode like a sack of potatoes, leaning this way and that. Somehow managed to stay aboard. If I'd seen this done to someone else, I might have thought it was funny.

I crawled away from the canyon rim and caught my mare. For the next hour, I rode from one end of the pasture to the other, looking for Grampy, but I didn't find him. He'd gotten lost in that maze of canyons and ravines. I could only hope that old Snips would find his way home . . . and that Grampy could stay upright in the saddle.

Unknown to Grampy and me, at ten o'clock that morning, while we were gone, a car pulled up in front of our house, a big fancy green Buick that belonged to our neighbors, the Tinsleys. The driver was one of the Tinsley cowboys, and in the backseat rode Mrs. Tinsley—dressed, as always, in fine clothes from her favorite store in Kansas City.

Mother had been gathering eggs and Coy was scattering some grain for the chickens when the car door opened and Mrs. Tinsley stepped out, helped by the driver.

Mother was surprised but cordial. "Why, Mrs. Tinsley, what a nice surprise."

They exchanged pleasantries and then Mrs. Tinsley said, "Dearie, I wondered if you'd mind if I looked at the house."

"The house? Well, I . . . yes, I suppose so, but it's a little messy. I wasn't expecting company."

Mrs. Tinsley started toward the house. "Don't you worry about it. I didn't give you any warning. I just wanted to see what it might need."

This made no sense to Mother, and after Mrs. Tinsley had walked through every room in the house, looking into every closet and cabinet, it made even less sense. Out on the porch, after the tour, Mrs. Tinsley said, "You've done so much with the place, Sara. It's just a shame . . . well, you know. We're very sorry, but our foreman needs a bigger place."

"I don't know what you mean, Mrs. Tinsley."

Mrs. Tinsley stared at Mother, her mouth half-open. Then she walked quickly toward the car. "Thank you, Sara. I'm sorry for the bother. Your house is really precious."

She dived into the backseat and the Buick drove away.

Coy looked up at Mother. "What was that all about?"

"I don't have the slightest idea. It was almost as though she thought . . . we were leaving."

I made it back to the house around noon. Coy heard me ride in and came running out to meet me.

"Where's Grampy?"

"I don't know. He's not back yet?"

Coy shook his head and whispered, "No, but the sheriff's here."

"Thank goodness!"

Mother came out on the porch, followed by Sheriff

Jake South, a smallish man who wore a black frock coat, high-topped boots with the pant legs tucked inside, and a big flat-brimmed hat that pushed down on his ears. He'd been sheriff of Hemphill County for as long as anyone could remember, but he never wore a gun.

Mother saw that I'd come back alone. "Riley, where's your grandfather?"

I heaved a sigh and shook my head. "Mother, you won't believe this."

Just then, we heard a horse approaching from the north. We all turned and saw . . . old Snips walking into headquarters, with Abner Dawson sitting backward in the saddle. Grampy wasn't hurt, but he looked about as mad and humble as a man could be.

Chapter Six

AROUND THE DINING table, we all listened as Grampy told the story about the moonshiners. He concluded by saying, "I guess they didn't like my music."

Coy and I smiled at that. Mother patted his hand and said, "Oh Daddy, you poor thing!"

Grampy looked over to Sheriff South. "Well, Jake, I guess you came at the right time. How'd you hear about all this?"

The sheriff's face grew very solemn. "I didn't. And I'm afraid I've got some bad news." He reached into the inside pocket of his coat and handed Grampy a piece of paper. "That's an eviction notice, signed by your sister. You've got thirty days to vacate the ranch."

We all stared at him, speechless. *Aunt Mattie was throwing us off the ranch?*

Mother, Coy, and I waited on the porch while Grampy followed the sheriff out to his car. "Now Jake, this is some kind of crooked deal."

"Read the document, Abner. It was signed in your sister's hand."

"Mattie wouldn't do that. I've had a few spats with her over the years, but she wouldn't take it out on my daughter."

"Abner, it's all legal and proper. There's not a thing I can do about it."

By the time they reached the car, we could hear anger rising in Grampy's voice. "You know, Jake, it seems a little funny that all this is happening at the same time, and I smell a rat. There's a lot of money in this moonshine business, but I never thought they could buy *you*."

They had reached the car. Sheriff South turned a pair of cold blue eyes on Grampy. "Let me explain something. I don't have any control over the U.S. Congress or the state of Texas. Nobody asked my opinion on this Prohibition business. I'm sheriff of one county with eight hundred people in it. I know that some of those folks are making whiskey to keep food on the table. As long as they pay their taxes, I leave 'em alone. I don't have the time or the funds to enforce laws the people don't respect."

Grampy was trying to keep his temper under control. "Uh . . . Jake, we ain't talking about poor farmers trying to buy groceries. That outfit in the canyon is a professional deal from the outside. I saw three men and didn't know any of 'em. They're not from around here. Now, they're breaking the law and they're a threat to my daughter and her boys. The question is, what are you going to do about it?"

The sheriff cut a slice of chewing tobacco off his plug. "And the answer is . . . nuthin'. Oh, I could make a raid, bust up their distills, throw 'em in jail at county expense. And you know what? In two days they'd be right back in business because . . ." He jabbed Grampy in the chest with his finger. ". . . the judges have been bought and the district attorney won't prosecute my cases. It stinks, Abner, the whole thing stinks to high heaven."

The sheriff cooled down for a minute. "Abner, me and you go back a long ways. We've been friends, and I've even had you in my jailhouse a few times."

"Uh . . . let's skip over that."

"You know I'm not crooked. My hands are tied and there's nothing I can do. I'm not your problem. Your problem's in Sparrow, Texas, and I'd suggest you start by talking to your sister." He climbed into the car and started the engine. "Tell your daughter that I'm sorry about all this. Good luck."

He drove away, leaving us in a cloud of dust. Mother left the porch and joined Grampy at the yard gate. "Can they actually do this? Throw us off the ranch and out of our home?"

Grampy's face was grim. "I don't know, sugar, but it seems that I need to make a trip to Sparrow."

"What about Forth Worth?"

Grampy managed a smile. "I guess Forth Worth will have to wait, won't it?"

I stepped forward. "I'd like to go with you. Monday's the last day of school."

Then Coy had to open his big yap. "And if Riley gets to go, so do I."

Grampy looked at Mother. "I guess that's up to your momma."

Mother's answer was, "No. Absolutely not."

She was adamant about not letting me go with Grampy, but I was determined to change her mind. That night, after supper, I cleared the dishes off the table, while Mother did some sewing and Coy washed dishes. He wore one of Mother's aprons that was five sizes too big, and he was such a peewee, he had to stand on a wooden apple crate to put the dishes away in the cabinet over the sink.

"Mother, be reasonable," I said. "Grampy might need some help."

"No."

I groaned and delivered the last load of dishes to Coy. I peeked around him and looked into the sink. "You do good work, O Little One."

"Shut your gob, Riley. And stop calling me that."

Mother looked up from her sewing. "Boys, that's enough."

I picked up one of the three kerosene lamps we had

burning in the house and walked over to a mirror on the wall. I held up the lamp and studied my face. I was looking for something in particular . . . and I found it.

I rushed over to Mother and pointed to my chin. "Mother, look at this!"

She squinted. "What?"

Coy had joined us by then, dribbling soapy water all the way from the sink. "What is it?"

"It's a whisker, my first black whisker! In one month, I'll look like Rutherford B. Hayes!"

Coy shook his head and went back to the sink. "Riley, you are so full of prunes."

"Mother, this settles it. I'm a grown man now and you should let me go with Grampy."

She gave me a sweet smile. "No."

"Mother, you just don't understand!" I stalked over to the screen door and looked out at the night. Down at the barn, I could see the yellow glow of Grampy's lantern and could hear him playing a sad tune on the fiddle. "Mother, what would we do if we had to leave the ranch?"

She looked up at the ceiling and sighed. "I don't know, Riley. We'll just have to hope that Daddy can . . ."

She didn't finish her thought. She was worried, and so was I. All at once we found ourselves depending on Abner Dawson, and that was a little bit scary.

Chapter Seven

At SIX-THIRTY on Monday morning, Coy and I kissed Mother good-bye, grabbed our lunches, and started our ride to school. It was a five-mile journey.

Laura Higgins was waiting for us at the usual spot. She and I rode together, while Coy tagged along behind. She asked about my weekend and I told her all the news: Grampy had come back, our encounter with the moonshiners, the eviction notice . . .

Laura was shocked. "Thrown off your ranch! Can they do that? Oh, Riley, this is terrible! Your poor mother!"

"But see, I could help, if she'd let me go with

Grampy. If you ask me, she's being totally unreason-able."

I could see Laura's eyes shifting into her Stern Adult Woman's glare. She did that well, and fairly often. "She's not being unreasonable at all, Riley. Let you and Coy go running off to a town full of outlaws and bootleggers?"

"Forget Coy. He can stay home."

"All right, then you. You're her oldest child and . . . Riley, you and Coy are all she has left in the world. Of course she's not going to let you go chasing off with your grandfather!" I couldn't think of a good response, so I let the subject drop. After a bit, Laura said, "Oh, by the way, Daddy was up late last night and happened to see a vehicle parked at the school. He saw the head-lights. It was three o'clock in the morning."

"He could see lights at the school? From your house?"

She gave me a patient smile. "Riley, we live on the prairie. We can see twenty miles in any direction."

"But three o'clock in the morning?"

"Yes, and it wasn't Miss Cates. Daddy got out his binoculars. It was a truck."

"A truck? Why would a truck be parked at the school?"

Laura shrugged. "Daddy wondered too. He thinks it has something to do with the whiskey business."

This was the last day of school. Miss Cates had some crazy notion that she could cram a few last bits of precious education into our skulls, and against huge odds, she gave it a try. She managed to keep order in the school through the first two hours of the morning, but it didn't last. Thirty-five restless, squirmy children proved to be a force like water rushing to the sea, and at ten-thirty she gave up, closed her history book, and surrendered to the chaos.

We spent the rest of the morning cleaning the school: sweeping the floor, washing the blackboard, cleaning the erasers, and packing books. While Miss Cates and a group of the younger kids were washing the blackboard, I found myself wondering if I could bean Jackie Tinsley on the head with a spitwad. It seemed the proper thing to do, since the Tinsleys had their greedy eyes on our ranch.

I built a nice juicy one and sent it flying across the room. It was my bad luck that a little girl named Amy walked into its path and took a direct hit on the cheek. She saw who did it and told the teacher. Miss Cates seemed almost pleased that I'd been caught in a crime, and she was smiling when she called me to the front.

"Riley, it appears that you don't have enough chores to occupy your mind, so while the other children go outside for lunch, you may stay inside and clean the ashes out of the stove. I want it spic and span."

A big coal-burning stove sat in the center of the school and was our only source of heat in the winter. Cleaning the stove was a dirty, unpleasant job, and I felt that a terrible injustice had been done. While the other kids played and laughed outside, I swept soot and cinders off the floor around the stove.

But sweeping the floor was the easy part. After I'd finished that, I had to open the door on the stove and clean out the inside, which meant scooping ashes into the ash bucket with a little coal shovel. That was nasty work, far beneath a man of my age and dignity.

I opened the little door in the middle of the stove and was surprised to see . . . no ashes inside. It appeared that somebody had already cleaned it. I knelt down and peered inside . . . and got a second surprise. There, at the back of the stove, was a white canvas sack.

I reached inside the stove and felt it. It was full of something heavy. I dropped the shovel, reached both hands inside, and dragged it out. It hit the floor with a clunk. I untied the string at the top and opened it up . . . and couldn't believe what I saw.

It was filled with twenty-dollar coins!

There must have been five thousand dollars in that sack!

For a minute or two, I just sat there, staring into the sack and wondering if I was dreaming, but then I heard footsteps on the wooden porch. In a flash, I stuck one of the coins into my pocket, tied the sack, placed it back into the stove, and slammed the little door shut.

When Miss Cates walked into the school, I was sweeping away with the broom, and even whistling a little tune—a perfect example of a young man who was happy at work.

"Spic and span?" She came toward the stove, her black "grandma shoes" clacking on the wood floor. She examined the floor. "Not bad, Riley. How about the inside?"

This caught me off guard. She bent over and reached for the little door. In desperation, I thrust out my hand.

"Miss Cates, I'd like to shake your hand. You've sure been a good teacher this year."

She gave me a suspicious look. But then her face softened. She smiled and shook my hand.

"Well, thank you, Riley. We've had a few differences this year, but . . . thank you. This was my first year of teaching, you know."

"Yes ma'am, and you were truly outstanding. Is there anything else you'd like for me to do for you?"

She studied me with her hawkish teacher-eyes. She was *really* suspicious now! "Riley, you surprise me, but . . . yes, as a matter of fact, I have some books . . ."

She left the stove and I heaved a sigh of relief and followed her over to her desk. There, she had several wooden apple crates filled with books. I carried them out to her automobile and loaded them into the rumble seat.

Not only did I manage to keep my secret safe, but Miss Cates pronounced me a "good boy" and gave me a piece of toffee candy. It was one of my finest moments.

After lunch, we played Twenty Questions to pass the time until three o'clock, when we would be dismissed for the day and for the year. I had trouble concentrating on the game. My thoughts were on that sack of gold that somebody had hidden in our stove. I couldn't imagine who could have put it there.

It must have been around two o'clock when we heard the car pull up in front of the school. Coy was leading the whole school in the Battle of Twenty Questions. Two doors slammed. Miss Cates frowned and went to the door at the back of the school. Two men stepped inside and spoke to Miss Cates in low voices. One of them was tall and wore a vested suit and tie. The other was an older man, rather small, wearing a black frock coat and a big Stetson hat that mashed down on his ears.

I recognized the older man. It was Jake South, our county sheriff.

At first, I didn't pay much attention to the other man . . . until I noticed that he reached into his coat pocket and brought out a *peanut*. And that's when I knew that this was the same man who had been in our canyon the day before—Joe.

And when I figured that out, I felt prickles of fear on the back of my neck.

I turned my eyes to the front and stared at the wall. I could hear my heart racing. I knew in a flash that his presence at the school had something to do with those coins in the stove. I could feel beads of sweat popping out in my hair and under my eyes.

Miss Cates walked to the front. Her lips were thin, and she had a look of concern in her eyes. The big man came behind her, his eyes prowling the room, while Sheriff South leaned against the wall and jingled the keys that hung on his belt. His gaze wandered and he looked bored.

Miss Cates stood with her heels together and clasped her hands in front of her. "Students, this is Mr. Joe McGreggor. He's a constable in Sparrow and he has some questions for us."

My head came up. *Constable?* Things were beginning to fit together.

Mr. McGreggor turned to us and flashed a two-second smile. "Hi. Students, I'm working a case that involves some stolen money. It was taken from a citizen of Sparrow and we have reason to think it might have been hidden somewhere in this neighborhood. Do any of you have any information that might help us in our investigation?"

I could hear my heart thumping in the silence. Maybe that man was a constable, but I knew he couldn't be trusted. Would I tell him about the coins? Not on your life.

The constable narrowed his eyes and searched every face in the room. When he came to mine, I was sure he would see GUILT written all over it in big letters, and he would notice that a drop of sweat was sliding down my forehead. His eyes locked on me and he spoke.

"I guess not. If you hear or see anything, I hope you'll let us know at once. I'll leave my card with Miss Cronin."

"Cates."

". . . with Miss Cates. She'll know how to get in contact with me. Thanks."

He flashed another two-second smile and started walking down the aisle. I could hear the floorboards squeaking under his feet. I didn't dare look at him. When he was right beside me, he stopped. I felt his hand touching my shoulder. I froze.

I'd been caught!

"You've got some soot on your shirt, sonny." He brushed it off and left the school.

I almost fainted with relief.

When they'd gone, Miss Cates picked up the peanut hulls he'd dropped on the floor. "You'd think an officer of the law would have better manners."

Chapter Eight

At three o'clock school was out for the summer. We said our good-byes and all the kids were celebrating. As we rode away from the school, Laura noticed that I was being unusually quiet. She said nothing for a while, but kept glancing at me, and finally she asked what was wrong.

I pulled the gold coin out of my pocket and showed her. Her eyes grew wide in amazement.

"I found a whole sack of them in the stove, but that's not all, Laura." I glanced over my shoulder to make sure Coy wasn't listening. He wasn't. "Constable McGreggor is involved with that whiskey still in our canyon. He's a crook, plain and simple, and that sack of gold has something to do with whiskey."

Laura blinked her eyes and caught her breath. "Oh my goodness."

"Which brings us to the very worst part. You were right about the truck at the school last night."

She laughed and gave her head a toss. "Try to remember that. But Riley, don't do anything foolish about that gold. It belongs to somebody, and they'll be watching it."

"Don't you worry. I might tell Grampy, but nobody else. I won't go near it . . . well, unless . . ."

"Riley, don't go near it! Leave it alone. Those men are gangsters."

"Yes ma'am."

When it was time for us to go our separate ways, I got down and opened the gate for Laura. She rode through the gate and I closed it.

"Oh, I had a thought about your mother. Had you considered inviting her to go on the trip to Sparrow? If she were along, she wouldn't worry about you boys, and I'll bet she would enjoy getting off the ranch."

I shook my head. "That's a bad idea. In the first place, she wouldn't go, and in the second place . . . Laura, she's my mother!"

"Yes. That's the point."

"I don't want to go off on a big adventure with my mother."

Laura smiled. "It was just a thought. Well, come

see us over the summer. I'll be anxious to hear how things turn out."

She waved her fingers and rode away. I was still watching her when Coy said, "You know, she's kind of pretty."

I threw the reins over Dolly's neck and climbed into the saddle.

We turned our horses south and started toward home. I noticed that Coy was looking at me out of the corner of his eye, and I figured he had something on his mind. He did.

"Riley, I want to know what you two were whispering about, and I don't appreciate you keeping secrets. I'm your brother, after all."

"All right, Mister Snoop, if you must know, we were talking about . . . farming."

He rolled his eyes up in his head. "Oh, you lie like a dog! Farming? Riley, it really hurts me that you think I'm dumb enough to believe that."

"All right, we were talking about the sack of gold I found in the school stove."

His head seemed to sink into his shoulders. "I'm going to tell Mother on you."

"Tell her what?"

"I'm going to tell her that every time I ask you a simple question, you give me this . . . this constant stream of lies, yarns, corn, and malarkey."

I had to laugh at him. "Coy, even when I tell the truth, you won't believe me. I don't know what to say to you anymore. Have you always been so suspicious of your fellow man?"

By now he was muttering and shaking his head. "It's you. You seem to take some kind of twisted pleasure in telling me stupid stories that nobody in this world would believe."

"Laura believed it."

"No she didn't. Laura Higgins would never believe a bunch of hooey about a sack of gold."

"Coy, I'm telling you, she believed it. And so should you. Maybe I'll tell Mother that you've become a suspicious little rat-face."

"Tell her, I don't care. She knows you tell whoppers all the time."

"What if I showed you a twenty-dollar gold piece?"

"Right now?"

"Right now. What would you give me? How about your saddle? We'll bet your saddle against my saddle."

He pressed his lips together. "All right, mister, I'll take that bet, and you'd better pay off too."

I reached into my pocket and, with a little fanfare, opened my palm. When Coy saw the gold coin, his mouth dropped open. He gave me a look of complete astonishment, collapsed over his saddlehorn, and let out a groan.

I laughed out loud. He was such a funny kid, always so serious about things. "Don't worry. You can keep the saddle. I wouldn't have a use for it anyway."

He cut his eyes at me. "I hate to take charity."

"It's not charity. If you rode bareback, I'd have to listen to you moan and complain."

He looked off to the horizon. "Okay, for you, I'll keep the saddle."

"Thank you, Coy."

"Did you really find a sack of gold in the stove?" I nodded. "Where'd it come from? Whose gold is it?"

"I don't know, but I'm betting it has something to do with bootleggers and moonshiners."

Coy's eyes grew wide and he whistled under his breath.

When we reached the house, I sent Coy down to the barn to unsaddle the horses, and I went into the house. I had some very important business to take care of. I found Mother sitting on the screened porch, sewing a button onto one of Coy's shirts. We exchanged pleasantries and then I went right to work. Pacing up and down in front of her, I launched into my case.

"Mother, I've come up with a plan."

"Riley, if it's about the trip to Sparrow . . ."

"Hear me out, Mother. This is the deal of the year, the deal of the century, and here it is. You'll go with us." Her eyes came up from her work. I plunged on. "Number one: if you're with us, you won't have to worry about me and Coy, right? Number two: you need a vacation."

"Riley, if I needed a vacation, I wouldn't go to that place."

"Mother, Sparrow's a city! It's got stores. You could shop, buy a new dress. And libraries. Bookstores. You want us to read, yes? Well, there you are. Coy would love it, and it would help expand our . . . our cultural horizons. And you'd have a chance to visit with Aunt Mattie."

She leaned back in the chair and gave me an odd little smile. "Riley, did you think of this yourself?"

"Sure. Yes. Of course. Well, maybe Laura . . ."

"Ah!"

"Mother, please!"

She put her sewing down. "Actually, I think it's a good idea."

"You do?"

"The only trouble is that we'd be riding in Daddy's truck. What if it rained? He doesn't have a cab on that thing, only a canvas top."

"Mother, it won't rain, I guarantee it. Start packing. I'll go tell Grampy."

I went flying out the door. I had notched up another victory! We were going to Sparrow!

I ran down to the barn. On the way, I noticed Grampy's truck parked outside. He and Spud Morris had gone into Canadian that morning and had brought it back.

I burst through the barn door. "Grampy, I've got it all settled."

He silenced me with a raised palm. He and Coy were standing at the east door of the barn, looking at something in the distance. I joined them and saw a very strange sight. Spud Morris, our hired man, was creeping around in the corral, about twenty yards away from the barn.

"What's he doing?"

Grampy shushed me again. "Shhh. Spud says he can pick up that skunk without getting sprayed. I'm betting a dollar that he can't."

I looked closer. Sure enough, Spud was creeping toward a skunk that was looking for bugs in the corral. The skunk didn't seem the least bit interested in Spud, and went on about his business.

Spud Morris was what you might call a solitary man. As far as I knew, he had no family or friends. He seemed content to stay out on our ranch and never seemed to crave the bright lights of town. He'd been working for us for as long as I could remember, and I guess he thought of us as his family.

He spoke with a stutter, and when he got excited about something, it got worse. If you weren't careful, he would spray you with spit as he struggled to get his words out. Mother thought the stuttering had started in his childhood, when his ears were damaged by an infection.

It didn't matter to us that he stuttered, or that he couldn't hear well. He had a pure heart, and was as loyal as a man could be.

All at once, Spud broke into a run and snatched up the skunk by his tail. Holding the skunk out at arm's length, he turned to us and yelled, "S-s-see? I d-d-done it!"

The skunk didn't spray. Spud carried him off a ways and pitched him out of the corral. Grampy grumbled, "Well, old Spud'll surprise you. He said a skunk can't spray when you've got him by the tail, and I guess he knew what he was talking about."

Spud came up to the door, wearing a big grin. "I t-t-told you, A-abner. D-didn't I t-t-tell you I could d-d-do it, do it?"

Grampy fished a dollar bill out of his jeans and slapped it into Spud's hand. "Spud, I think you cheated, but I'll pay off."

"No sir, d-d-didn't cheat. I used to m-m-make my l-l-living s-selling hides, hides."

"Well, that's a form of cheating. You withheld important information, see."

Spud cackled. "Y-you're just m-m-mad 'cause you l-l-lost, huh huh."

Chuckling to himself, Spud went out into the horse pasture to bring in his milk cow, Petunia.

Coy went with Spud, leaving me and Grampy alone. Grampy turned to me. "Now, you came busting in here with some kind of news. What was it?"

I told him about my conversation with Mother, and that we were all going with him to Sparrow. Then I pulled the gold coin out of my pocket and showed it to him. He took it and turned it over in his fingers. He even bit it to see if it was a lead slug.

"Son, where in the world did you find this?"

"There's a whole sack of them in the stove at school. Oh, and you remember the big man you met in the canyon, the one they called Joe? Well, he showed up at school today, and guess who he is."

"Buffalo Bill."

"No. He's Constable McGreggor . . . from Sparrow! And he was looking for that money."

Grampy narrowed his eyes and studied the floor for a long time. "Well sir, we have lots of questions for my sister, don't we? Something mighty strange is going on around here." He handed me the coin. "Tell my daughter that I'm pulling out of here at eight o'clock sharp. If she's not ready, she stays home. I hate to wait on a woman—even a nice one like your momma."

Chapter Nine

GRAMPY HAD MADE such a big issue out of leaving promptly at 8:00 the next morning, I made sure that Coy, Mother, and I were packed, loaded, and ready to roll. At 7:59 Mother was sitting in the front seat, and Coy and I were sprawled on bedrolls in the back.

We were ready to go. But Grampy wasn't, and neither was his truck. He'd found some problem in the engine's electrical system.

At ten o'clock, two hours later, Grampy and Spud were still banging tools and working on the problem. Grampy had cursed the truck in fifteen languages and was so mad he could hardly speak. Coy had fallen asleep and Mother had scooted down in the seat, listening with a wry smile to Grampy's muttering and clanging.

I watched the whole thing. When Grampy and Spud worked together, it was always hilarious. They fought like cats and dogs.

Grampy was under the hood, poking around with wrenches and screwdrivers. He had spent the first hour muttering and snarling about the stupidity of everyone who worked at the Ford Motor Company. After that, he had shifted into a more ominous form of anger—silent white-lipped, pinch-eyed rage, which exceeded his ability to express it through screams.

Spud stood at the front of the truck with the crank in his thick hands.

Grampy yelled, "All right, Spud, give 'er a twirl and we'll see if she's getting spark. No, wait just a . . ."

Spud didn't hear the second part, only the "give 'er a twirl" part. He put his back into the job and spun the motor. A howl of pain came from under the hood. Grampy had been touching the magneto wire and had gotten a shock. He rolled off the fender and landed in a heap on the ground. The motor chugged, sputtered, and started running.

Spud beamed a smile. "She's w-w-working, A-abner!"

Grampy picked himself up off the ground and wiped his hands on his jeans. Then he beamed Spud a glare full of daggers and yelled over the noise of the motor, "Spud, when you show up to help, it's just like three good men quit!"

Spud cupped a hand around his ear. "Wh-what did you s-s-say?"

Grampy slapped his hat on his head and dived into the driver's seat. "I said, get out of the road! I don't want to be tempted to run you over." He gunned the motor, put her in gear, and we lurched forward. Spud jumped out of the way, and as we drove past, Grampy yelled, "Check the windmills and don't forget to feed the horses!"

We roared out of the driveway in front of the house, scattering Mother's laying hens in all directions. We were off on our big adventure.

Coy sat up and yawned and looked around. "Good grief, what took us so long?" I pointed to Grampy. Coy nodded and went back to sleep.

The roads in our part of the world weren't very good and the seventy-mile trip to Sparrow usually required four to six hours. The first two-mile stretch was little more than a two-rut trail through our Mesa pasture. At our south fence line, I got out and opened the gate and we entered the Tinsley ranch, and followed another pasture trail two miles to the river road. This road ran parallel to the Canadian River, whose broad green meadows lay just to the south of us. The river road carried more traffic than the pasture trails and had been improved somewhat, but it was still as rough as a washboard.

Now and then I caught a glimpse of Mother—holding her hat against the wind, fanning dust with her hand, and groaning at all the bumps in the road. She never did reach the point of telling Grampy to slow down, but I could see that it crossed her mind several times.

Around noon, we drove up to Rudolph Lehman's little house on the north side of the river. Mr. Lehman was an old German bachelor who kept a team of good Belgian horses and used them to pull vehicles across the boggy Canadian River. Grampy paid him the two-dollar fee and Mr. Lehman's horses did their job, towing the truck across to the other side.

The rest of the trip was uneventful, except that between the towns of Pampa and Sparrow, we ran into a thunderstorm. In the back of the truck, Coy and I took cover beneath a canvas tarp, while Mother, riding in the windowless cab, covered herself with a wool blanket.

Over the roar of the rain, I heard her say, "I knew this would happen, Riley McDaniels! My hair's going to be a scandal!"

But the rain didn't last long. The sun popped out of the clouds and we continued our journey, with Grampy plowing a path through the muddy road. Then, around four o'clock, Grampy stopped the truck on a hill, and we looked down on the wicked city of Sparrow, Texas.

Chapter Ten

JUST A YEAR ago, it had been nothing but an empty pasture and a dream in the mind of Uncle George Sparrow. Oil had been discovered, huge wells that flowed ten thousand barrels of oil a day, and within weeks people had poured in from other boomtowns in Texas and Oklahoma—speculators, investors, drillers, rig hands, boilermakers, toolpushers, truckers, carpenters, rig builders, and teamsters.

Shacks and crude sheet iron buildings went up as fast as material could be freighted from the railroad at Panhandle City, thirty miles to the south. Workers lived in cot houses, in tents, in their cars, in wooden packing crates. Other simply slept in alleys or on the lease sites where they worked.

Right behind the oil field workers came merchants who threw up boxy square-front store buildings on the main streets: dry goods, hardware, pawnshops, cafes, hotels, boardinghouses, gas stations, grocery stores, lumberyards, and oil field supply stores. And behind the merchants came the shady element we had heard so much about: gamblers, pickpockets, thieves, moonshiners, bootleggers, dance hall girls, bank robbers, swindlers, con men, and crooks of every description.

Grampy waved his hand across the sprawl of the town. "Five thousand people live down there, and they all came here to get rich. Some did and some didn't. Mattie's husband was one who did."

A team and wagon had come up behind us, and the teamster stood up and yelled for us to move on. Grampy leaned out and looked back at the team, then he released the hand brake and we started coasting down the hill.

"That man behind us has four of the prettiest Percheron horses you'll ever see. It kind of pleases me to find that motor trucks haven't put the horse out of business."

We drove toward the center of town and stared out at the things we'd never seen before: wooden derricks, huge wooden tanks, gas flares, and then row after row of wooden homes, all the same size and shape.

By then, we had caught the smell of Sparrow. The odor of oil and gas hung heavy in the air. Grampy noticed that Coy and I had wrinkled our noses. "Boys, what you're smelling is money."

We came to Main Street and stared at the teeming mass of humanity. Cars lined the curbs on both sides of the street, which had been turned into a swamp of mud by the rain and traffic. Two cars were stuck in the middle of the street and gangs of men were pushing them through the mud. A banner stretched across the street advertised DANCING AT THE OASIS in huge black letters, and right below it a truck had spilled a load of pipe.

Men milled around on the edges of the traffic, going in and out of places with names such as Joe's Lunch, K.C. Store, Golden Eagle Tailor Shop, Hub Store, and Harvey Hardware, stepping around the barrels, boxes, and crates that were stacked high in front of the stores.

Mother said, "They're all men. I haven't seen one single woman."

Grampy lifted one brow. "Well, they're here, honey, I can promise you that. Where there's a bunch of men, the ladies aren't far away." He scowled at the maze of traffic. "You know, I think we'll just park this thing and walk to Mattie's place. I don't think my nerves can stand all this traffic."

He pulled onto a side street and parked. We climbed out and stretched our legs. Mother slapped the road dust off her dress. We, being accustomed to silence in our canyon, suddenly realized that there was no silence in Sparrow. The air was filled with the shouts and laughter of men, the hum of motors, the distant hiss of gas flares, and the clanging of drilling rigs pounding their sharpened tools into the earth.

Mother turned to Grampy and said, "Do you know where we're going?"

"Certainly. To my sister's house."

"Do you have an address?"

"No."

She placed one hand on her hip and glared at him. "Daddy, why didn't you get an address? We'll have to ask for directions."

His hand came up. "No. We'll find it. She lives in the biggest house in town. Besides, we're not in any big rush. Let's give these boys a look at a Texas boom-town."

And so we began our walk down the main street of this bustling town. We must have looked like the country folk we were—reading every sign, looking into every store window, staring at every man in over-alls that had been splashed with oil on the job.

We had walked and gawked our way down the first two blocks, when we heard men shouting behind us. Their voices were angry, and they grew louder. We turned and saw two rough-looking men facing each other in the middle of the street.

"Give me my money, you weasel!"

"Come and get it, if you're man enough!"

Traffic came to a stop and a crowd gathered. Drivers left their cars, grinning in anticipation of a fistfight. But the men didn't plan to use their fists. Out came two pistols and they started blazing away at each other—in the middle of Main Street, in the middle of the day!

When the first shots rang out, the crowd scattered and Grampy herded us out of the street and toward a store called The Mercantile. Right behind us came a stray bullet that passed through the store's open front window.

Suddenly, the door opened and a dark-eyed man stepped out and said, "In here, quick!"

We dived into the store.

The stranger told us to hide behind the counter, while he crept back to the door. He opened it a crack and peered out. The shooting stopped. He closed the door and came over to the counter, shaking his head.

He was a nice-looking man with piercing black eyes, wavy black hair, and olive skin. He wore good-fitting clothes: trousers, a white shirt and tie, and a dark vest. A gold watch chain looped across the vest. He looked us over, one by one, and smiled, revealing a beautiful set of teeth.

"You're not from here, I judge. I thought you might appreciate getting in out of the . . ." He rolled his hand in the air. ". . . excitement."

Grampy adjusted his hat, which had gotten cocked to the side, and hitched up his pants. "You judged right, friend. We're not from here and we're not fond of that kind of adventure. Many thanks."

The man offered his hand. "I'm Aaron Kaplan."

Grampy shook his hand and introduced us all.

Then, with a grin, he said, "Do y'all do this sort of thing every day?"

Mr. Kaplan laughed. "I'm afraid it happens fairly often. Sparrow is still a raw town."

"Well, I guess it worked out all right. Did anybody get shot?"

"No, they were drunk and were never much danger to each other."

Mother had been watching him, and she said, "Mr. Kaplan, how did you know we weren't from here? Do we look . . . country?"

He clasped his hands together, with both index fingers pointed up. "No ma'am. You look wholesome."

Grampy chortled. "Wholesome, huh? Well, you look kind of wholesome yourself, son, and from the way you talk, I'd guess you're not from here either."

"I've lived in many places. My business requires it." Just then, the bell over the front door jingled and a large man wearing a suit walked in.

"Afternoon, Mr. Kaplan," he said. "I was in the neighborhood and thought you might want to contribute to the Widows and Orphans Fund."

When Mr. Kaplan saw him, his face darkened. "Excuse me a moment."

I stared at the stranger, then leaned over to Mother and whispered, "That's the man who came to our school! That's Constable McGreggor!"

When Grampy recognized the constable, he hid behind the counter.

Mr. Kaplan went to the cash register and counted

out ten one-dollar bills. While he was doing that, the constable came walking over to us, looking us over with intrusive eyes.

"Where are you-all from?"

Mother said, "Out of town."

"Oh? Where?"

"Hemphill County."

"You don't say." The constable reached into his coat pocket and pulled out a peanut. "Pretty country. I was there not so long ago. What brings you to Sparrow?"

"Family business."

The constable cracked the peanut, popped the nuts into his mouth, and let the shells fall to the floor. "That's nice." He walked back to Mr. Kaplan, held out his hand, and took the money. "Many thanks, Mr. Kaplan. The widows and orphans of this town are grateful."

The bell over the door jingled and he walked out.

Grampy came out of hiding, and so did Mr. Kaplan's clerk, a man named Tim, who had hit the floor when the shooting started. He looked pale and shaken.

When Mr. Kaplan returned to us, he studied us with curious eyes. "Do you know our Constable Mc-Greggor?"

We all traded glances, then Grampy said, "We're acquainted. Is he a friend of yours?"

Mr. Kaplan laughed, and you'd have to say that it was a bitter laugh. "No, he's not a friend. Listen. Why don't you come upstairs to my apartment where we can talk?" He smiled at Mother. "You might want to freshen up after your trip."

Mother nodded, realizing that the rain and wind had done bad things to her hair.

We followed Mr. Kaplan through the store, past tables covered with shirts, pants, and overalls, and racks filled with coats, jackets, and vests on hangers. The farther we went, the darker the store became. As we passed a big coal stove, Mr. Kaplan started up a wooden stairway that turned to the left halfway up. Each step had a distinctive squeak.

At the top of the stairs he came to a door. He jingled a set of keys, inserted one, and opened the door. Light poured through the opening, illuminating his face for a moment. He seemed cautious or worried. He motioned for us to follow. We climbed the last four steps and walked into his living quarters.

What we saw inside surprised us all.

Chapter Eleven

"I APOLOGIZE FOR the room," said Mr. Kaplan. "I live alone and wasn't expecting company."

Coy and I traded glances. We couldn't see anything that might have deserved an apology. Mr. Kaplan's living quarters seemed a shocking contrast to the city around it—bright, clean, and orderly. And we noticed right away that he had electric lights, inside plumbing, and even a telephone. Our house back at the ranch had none of those conveniences.

Light flooded into the windows which were framed with drapes made of some elegant fabric, maybe velvet, dark green. There was a large four-poster bed, neatly made; several heavy upholstered sitting chairs; and a coffee table made of rich hardwood, with legs that were carved into swirls and patterns. Upon the table were a large ashtray and a pipe, and near them, a violin and bow.

Grampy noticed the violin right away.

Nearby stood a large desk and chair upon a colorful rug, and occupying the entire north wall, dwarfing and dominating everything else in the room, was an *entire library*—row after row of books, shelf after shelf of books, hundreds of books, from floor to ceiling.

Coy gaped at it with wondering eyes and an open mouth. Mother did the same, and said, "Oh my!"

Mr. Kaplan smiled. "Books are a vice of mine, as you see. It's not very practical for a man who moves about." Mother continued to stare at the books. Coy walked toward them, as though approaching a holy shrine, his mouth still hanging open. Mr. Kaplan seemed amused. "It's not a bad collection."

At last Coy found his voice. "I've never seen so many books! Our county library doesn't have this many books." He turned his wide eyes to Mr. Kaplan. "Where did you get them all?"

"Not around here, I'm afraid. I order from dealers in New York and Baton Rouge. They send me catalogs." He turned to Mother and gestured toward the chairs. "Won't you have a seat? We can talk." He turned back to Coy. "Look all you want, young man. Just put each book back where you found it."

"Yes sir. Thank you." We had lost my little brother.

Mr. Kaplan went to the window, glanced down at the street, and turned back to Mother and Grampy. "Now, how does it happen that visitors to our city know the constable? If you don't mind telling me, that is."

Grampy and mother held a silent conversation with their eyes. Then Grampy said, "Uh . . . maybe we ought to find out which side you're on, Mr. Kaplan."

"Fair enough. I'm a merchant, on the side of law and order, and my dislike of Constable McGreggor defies description."

Grampy nodded and pointed to me. "Tell him, son."

I began the story, starting with the moonshiners in our canyon and ending with Constable McGreggor's visit to our school. Mr. Kaplan listened without expression, but with keen interest. I felt that his dark eyes were looking straight into my mind.

He nodded and said, "A very interesting story. We'll return to it, but first I'll give you my perspective on Constable McGreggor. As you know, he's an officer of the law. What you might not know is that he's a very corrupt man, part of a web of corruption that holds this city in its grip. I met him the day I opened my store. He came to ask if I wanted to contribute to the so-called Widows and Orphans Fund.

"I declined. After three mysterious fires and several broken windows, I began . . . contributing, shall we say. It's become a cost of doing business in Sparrow. So! They're making whiskey on your ranch and selling it in Sparrow, and Constable McGreggor is right in the middle of it."

Mother nodded. "Your town has been taken over by gangsters, and so has our ranch."

"Exactly. We have a common enemy. What a fascinating coincidence!" He turned to me. "You've done some fine detective work, my boy, but I must tell you that you were lucky. These people are ruthless and have no conscience—all the more reason to get them off your ranch, yes?" He frowned and pressed his lips together. "How long will you be in town? And where are you staying?"

Mother and Grampy traded looks, and Grampy said, "Well, son, we came to visit kinfolks, but that can wait." Grampy gave Mr. Kaplan a cunning smile and pointed to the violin. "Who plays that thing?"

This seemed to catch Mr. Kaplan by surprise. "I play, or I attempt to play. I don't pretend to be a good musician."

"Uh-huh." Grampy leaned back in his chair, clasped his hands behind his neck, and threw a leg over his other knee. "Well, we probably can't leave until we hear you play."

Mr. Kaplan's dark eyes darted from Grampy to Mother. "I guess I could, if you insist." He picked up the fiddle and bow and adjusted the tuning. He rifled through some sheet music on the table. "What would you like to hear? Mozart? Chopin? Brahms?"

Grampy smirked. "Oh yes, any of those. You pick one."

Mr. Kaplan picked one and carried the music over to the window, where he pulled a music stand out of the corner. He placed the music on the stand, checked the tuning again, and started playing.

It was a kind of music I'd never heard before—very dignified, you might say, slow, precise, and just a little bit sad, but nice. It was very different from the kind of tunes Grampy played. Mr. Kaplan didn't jump around or tap his foot, as Grampy so often did, but I could see from the swaying of his body and the intensity of his expression that he had a deep feeling for the music.

When he finished, we all clapped, even Coy, who had drifted away from the library to listen. Mr. Kaplan seemed embarrassed by our applause.

Grampy plunked his boots on the floor and leaned forward with his elbows on his knees. "Son, that is *wonderful!* I'm sure you wouldn't mind playing us one more."

Mr. Kaplan brought out a gold pocket watch and snapped it open. "Well, I suppose I could. Are you sure?

Mother nodded. "Yes, please play some more."

"All right. If you can stand it, I suppose I can too."

"We can stand it," said Grampy. "I assure you."

Mr. Kaplan found another piece of music and played it. Grampy leaned forward and listened to every note. His eyes were shining with excitement, and he seemed to be watching every movement of Mr. Kaplan's fingers and bow. When he finished, we applauded. He set the fiddle and bow down on the table.

"Thank you. You're more than generous. I know I'm not that good."

Grampy was still glowing. "Son, it was fine! I've never heard a fiddle played just that way."

Mr. Kaplan looked at him for a moment. "Do you play?"

Grampy slumped back in his chair. "No."

Mother turned to him. "Daddy, shame on you. Tell the truth."

"Sugar, he's a *musician*. As far as he's concerned, I don't play."

"Daddy!"

I said, "Mr. Kaplan, he does play. Go on, Grampy, take the fiddle."

Grampy sank deeper into the chair. "No."

Mr. Kaplan picked up the fiddle and bow and handed them to him. "Please."

Grampy growled and grumbled, but Mother wasn't about to let him escape. At last he took the instrument and gave Mr. Kaplan his chair. He started playing a tune, but Mother interrupted him.

"Daddy, stop that! You sound like a wounded chicken. Play your own way and stop worrying about Mr. Kaplan. Put yourself into it and play just the way you'd play at home."

Grampy grumbled and muttered, but then he closed his eyes and followed Mother's advice. He tore into a breakdown number and played it his own way— tapping his foot, smiling on the sweet notes, moaning under his breath, and moving his upper body in time with the music. And he didn't bother to stop after the first tune, but went straight into another and another. The whole time, he never opened his eyes.

I stole glimpses of Mr. Kaplan. He seemed hypnotized. When Grampy quit, he leaped out of his chair and pulled Grampy into a hug. "My word, man, that's tremendous! It's astonishing! I don't have words . . . I should have known better than to play first. You've embarrassed me."

Grampy studied him. "Son, I've embarrassed *me*, not you."

"You played all that out of your head! You didn't need music."

"Well, there's a reason for that. I can't read music. Us who can't read have to play by ear, such as it is."

"No, no, you have it backward. Those of us who lack your intuitive sense must read notes on a page. It's mechanical work, anyone can do it. But you . . ." He turned to Mother. "He's fantastic. I've never heard such a performance." Back to Grampy. "Listen. I belong to a little group. We're meeting tonight. You *must* join us, I insist."

Grampy gave him a cautious look. "Are they musicians, like you?"

"Yes, like me, only better."

"Uh-oh. Forget that. I ain't about to expose myself in front of a bunch of real musicians."

Mr. Kaplan turned to Mother. "Please, Mrs. McDaniels. I can't tell you how much joy your father has brought me. My friends and I live in this town, surrounded on all sides by junk, noise, ugliness, and corruption. During the day, we peddle and sell and do our work, but our hearts cry out for beauty. At night, we find relief in our books and music. Please allow me to share your father with my friends."

"That's very nice," she said. "We would be delighted. But if we're going out in public, I need to do something with my hair."

Mr. Kaplan showed her the bathroom.

While we waited for Mother, Mr. Kaplan put a record on his phonograph machine, a piece of classical music by a German composer none of us had ever heard of—Richard Wagner. Grampy stood over the phonograph for a long time, watching the record spin around and listening to a woman singing in a loud and desperate voice.

After a while, he turned to Mr. Kaplan and said, "Is she dead yet?"

Mr. Kaplan laughed. He was with Coy in front of the library. He pointed to a shelf of books and said, "This is the history of Greece and Rome. This, ancient Egypt. The American Civil War. German literature and philosophy. English poets. Shakespeare and Jonson. Astronomy. Physics and mathematics. History and literature of the Jewish people. Russian authors. History of music and composers. American novels. What do you think?"

Coy was amazed. "Wow! Have you read them all?"

"Not all, no. I wasted a lot of money on the German philosophers. They're beyond me. Kant? Hegel? Ah!" He tossed his hand into the air.

"I've never even heard of them."

"Just as well. They'll break your head." Mr. Kaplan noticed that I was off to the side, watching and listening. "Riley, you're not interested in books?"

"No sir, not very. I can't seem to sit still long enough to finish one."

He reached up to one of the higher shelves and pulled out a volume. He brought it over and handed it to me. "This is the one for you, *Tom Sawyer*. It was written for boys who don't like to read. I'll loan it to you on two conditions. First, you must read it. And second, you must return it to my library. I'm very strict about getting my books back."

I took the book. I knew I would never read it, but I promised that I would return it.

Just then, the lady on the phonograph howled, and Grampy said, "There she went, that did it! She's dead now!"

Mr. Kaplan tilted his head to the side and smiled at Grampy. I'm sure he'd never met anyone like Abner Dawson.

Chapter Twelve

AFTER A SHORT while, Mother joined us in the sitting room, looking cheerful and fresh. Mr. Kaplan locked up the store and we started walking to the restaurant where the orchestra gathered one night a week.

On both sides we could hear loud player piano music pouring out of the dance halls and the clang of slot machine levers coming from gambling dens, along with bursts of laughter. One establishment, The Oasis, was particularly loud. Mr. Kaplan said it was probably the worst place in town. In the distance, we could hear the hiss of the gas flares, whose eerie light danced in the growing twilight.

We turned onto a side street and made our way toward an establishment whose sign bore a single word, Vladeck's. It gave no hint of what Vladeck did in his place. Customers who went there must have known in advance.

We were passing a street lamp when we noticed two men standing beneath it. Mr. Kaplan watched them closely, and then one of them spoke. "Out for a stroll, Mr. Kaplan?"

He held up his violin and said, "Orchestra."

"Ain't that nice."

We hurried on down the street. The man who had spoken was Constable McGreggor. Mr. Kaplan said nothing about it, but he seemed pensive.

Vladeck's turned out to be a restaurant, but not the kind you would have expected to find in the Texas Panhandle. Instead of the usual fare of fried steak, fried chicken, chicken and dumplings, and Texas dishes, Mr. and Mrs. Vladeck, who ran the place and appeared to be the only employees, served dishes that Mr. Kaplan called Eastern European: several types of sausage, corned beef, pastrami, sauerkraut, boiled cabbage, and dishes I'd never heard of before.

The menu was written on a small blackboard on the wall. None of our family knew what to order, so Mr. Kaplan ordered for all of us. The Vladecks delivered it in big steaming bowls. Grampy was suspicious of food he couldn't pronounce, and he sampled it in small bites. But he liked the taste, and was soon putting away large helpings. So were the rest of us.

There were other customers sitting nearby. Mr. Kaplan greeted them and we soon realized that they were his musician friends. They set aside one night a week to eat at Vladeck's, and then played music.

"Mr. Schultz runs a hardware store and plays viola. Mr. and Mrs. Pennington own a tobacco store. He plays cello, she plays violin. Dr. Frankel is a physician and plays the violin. Bernard Marks is a locksmith and plays violin. They're my friends." He turned to Mother. "Everyone in Sparrow isn't a gangster, and you see, we have women here too. The Vladecks play with us as well. He plays the bass, she the French horn."

At seven o'clock, Mr. Vladeck locked the front door, pulled down the shades, and pushed the tables over against the walls. The musicians brought out their instruments, pulled their chairs into a half-circle, and sat down. Mr. Marks, the locksmith, appeared to be the leader, and they all tuned to his violin. He called the piece of music they were to play, set the tempo, and they began playing.

It was another classical number, very dignified, sometimes slow and sometimes fast, sometimes melancholy and sometimes sweet. I was no judge of music, but it sounded good to my ears, and I couldn't help being impressed at their ability to play together as a group.

Grampy was fascinated. He sat forward on the edge of his chair, watching this instrument and that instrument, but paying special attention to the work of the violinists.

At one point, he turned to Mother and said, "Look at that little locksmith's vibrato. He has 'er down cold, don't he?" Mother nodded and told him to shush. Later, Grampy pointed to his ear and said, "I didn't know you could find four fiddle players in the whole world that could play in tune, but they are." Mother nodded and put her finger to her lips.

It was a long piece, lasting half an hour or more. At last they ended it, and we clapped as loudly as we could. They thanked us and smiled. They all seemed to be shy and quiet people. Then Mr. Kaplan held up his hands for silence.

"Now, ladies and gentlemen, we have a special treat. Put away your instruments and prepare to listen to my friend, Mr. Abner Dawson."

Grampy almost choked when he heard that. Maybe he thought Mr. Kaplan had forgotten about him, and all at once he looked scared. He pleaded with Mr. Kaplan to let him off the hook, but Mr. Kaplan was firm. Shaking his head and throwing looks of despair at Mother, Grampy trudged over to his fiddle case.

He plucked the strings and said they were out of tune, he would never get them back in tune, they sounded awful. Mother whispered something to him and it seemed to help. We waited. He tuned and tuned, took a deep breath of air, and faced the audience. He looked pale and solemn, not like Grampy at all. I was surprised. He had played in front of people all his life, but I'd never seen him so rattled.

"Good evening," he said in a weak voice. "It's been my great pleasure this evening to hear people who love music in a way I've never known, never understood, never even thought about." His voice trembled. "You know, I'd give anything in this world if I could play what y'all just played. I never heard such sweet sounds in my whole life. It makes me feel very humble, and I sure don't deserve to be up here. But I am, so . . . here goes."

He started playing, and right away Mother knew it was wrong. She shocked everyone by standing up and yelling—*yelling*, mind you, and my mother wasn't one to yell—she yelled out, "Daddy, stop coddling that fiddle and play it your own way! *Tear it up!*"

Grampy nodded. When she said, "Tear it up," he knew what she meant. He said, "Okay, sugar, hang on to your drawers." He closed his eyes, tapped his foot, and played "Fisher's Hornpipe" the way Abner Dawson knew how to play it.

He tore it to pieces! He tore it up and put it back together, played it upside down and played it backward. He sawed and pulled, dipped the bow and squeezed the sound, leaned forward, leaned back, jumped and hopped and pounded the wooden floor with his boot. Sweat glistened on his face, and he played with a smile that you would have to describe as sublime.

The musicians were transfixed. Not an eye moved until he pulled out the last note and finally let go of it. Then they broke into wild applause and came to their feet. Grampy didn't know how to respond. He gave them an awkward bow and tried to put away his fiddle, but they cried for more. He shrugged, flashed a grin, and tore up another one.

Before any of us knew what was happening, Mr. Vladeck was dancing with Mrs. Vladeck, Mr. Pennington with Mrs. Pennington, and Mr. Marks was dancing with Mr. Schultz. Aaron Kaplan turned to Mother and offered his hand. She blushed and glanced at us boys, then jumped up and danced.

I turned to Coy. "Well, do you want to dance with me?" He wrinkled up his nose and gave me a sour face, so I got up and found a mop against the wall, and danced with Molly Mop. I didn't know how to dance, but it was fun. Nobody could sit still when Grampy was hot on that fiddle.

After a couple of tunes, Mother asked me to dance. I handed Molly Mop to Mr. Kaplan and Mother and I made a few turns. Then she dragged Coy out on the floor and made him dance, and while I was laughing at Coy, Mrs. Vladeck tapped me on the shoulder and invited me to dance with her. She seemed such a sweet lady, I hated to expose her to my clodhopping, but I didn't have the courage to say no.

We did all right. She led and I followed.

Then Dr. Frankel brought out his fiddle and started playing a song that was very different. It wasn't classical and it wasn't the fiddle music Grampy played. It was a mournful, haunting melody. Grampy was fascinated by it. He listened for a while, got it in his mind, and started playing harmony. It was so pretty, it gave me cold chills.

But right in the middle of the song, there was a loud knock at the door. *Bang bang bang!* The music stopped and Mr. Vladeck went to the door and opened it. The door flew open, knocking Mr. Vladeck aside, and in walked Constable McGreggor.

He wore a smirk on his mouth and ran his gaze over the faces in the room. Grampy bent over and busied himself with his fiddle case so the constable wouldn't recognize him. The constable reached into his pocket and brought out a peanut.

"We've had complaints about the noise. Y'all better pack up and go home."

He walked out the door, leaving a peanut hull on the floor.

That killed the evening. The musicians packed up their instruments, thanked Grampy for coming, and slipped away into the night. Bernie Marks came up and shook Grampy's hand. "Bernie Marks. Fantastic. Come back some time."

Dr. Frankel was next in line. He shook Grampy's hand and handed him a business card. "Abe Frankel, Mr. Dawson. I'm a physician, if you should need my services. Thank you for sharing your talent with us."

Grampy shook his hand. "The pleasure was all mine, I assure you. Say, Doc, what was that song you were playing?"

"A Jewish song. My grandfather used to play it."

"Well, sir, that's a beautiful piece of music. Thank

you for letting me play with you. I hope I can remember those chords."

The doctor flashed one of his rare smiles, then turned to Aaron Kaplan and lowered his voice. "Thursday night, as planned? Be careful, my friend."

Later, as we made our way down the dark street, Grampy turned to Mr. Kaplan. "Are those people Jewish?"

"Mr. Marks and Dr. Frankel. I'm also Jewish."

Grampy didn't know what to say at first. "Well, son, I've read about you folks all my life, and I'm honored to finally meet one of the Children of Israel. I sure admire what y'all did to old Pharaoh."

Mr. Kaplan laughed. "We had help on that one."

"I didn't know Jewish people lived around here."

"You'd be surprised, Mr. Dawson. There were Jews in this country before the Revolutionary War. There were Northern Jews who fought in the Civil War against Southern Jews who owned slaves. There were Jewish cowboys, ranchers, farmers, miners, trappers, and Indian scouts. Every city west of the Mississippi has a Jewish community, and I would venture that every boomtown in America has had its Jewish citizens."

"Huh. Well, your friends sure make fine music."

"Thank you." Aaron snapped open his watch. "It's almost eleven o'clock. Had you folks made arrangements for the night?"

Grampy explained that we had planned to stay with Aunt Mattie Sparrow. "But as late as it is, maybe we'd better find a hotel. Do you know my sister?"

"Well, not personally, but everyone here knows *of* the Sparrows. Did I hear that she's been sick?"

"If Mattie's been sick, I'd be the last to know. We have . . . differences."

"Well, all the hotels will be full of day-shift workers. Would you consider staying the night at my place?"

In the distance, we heard shouting and the crash of broken glass. Mother said, "I think that would be a very good idea. Thank you."

When we came to The Mercantile, Aaron slipped his key into the door lock, but before opening the door, he leaned down and pulled a match stick out of the crack between the door and the jamb. He motioned for us to wait, while he went inside and found a light.

Upstairs in his apartment, he told us to make ourselves at home. "I'll be downstairs, if you need anything."

As he turned to leave, Grampy caught him by the arm. "Son, what causes a man to leave a matchstick wedged in his door?"

And Mother said, "And why did that constable break up your gathering? I can't believe he got any complaints about the noise."

Aaron was thoughtful for a moment, then came inside and closed the door.

Chapter Thirteen

HE WALKED OVER to the window, parted the curtains, and looked down on the street. Then he faced us.

"Those people you met tonight are merchants, like me. We all have the same problem: we're trying to live honest lives in a town that has been seized by gangsters. In public, we're known as the town orchestra. Behind closed doors, we're a group of citizens who are determined to make Sparrow a decent, law-abiding town. And we're being watched."

Mother frowned. "Watched? What do you mean?"

"I mean," Aaron flopped down in one of the stuffed chairs, "that every public official, every police officer is corrupt, and most have criminal records. I'm sure that's hard for you to grasp, but it's the truth. If our group succeeds, those gangsters will go to prison, so the stakes are high. They sometimes search my store, which is why I leave a match in the door."

We were all silent for a moment, then Mother said, "That sounds a little frightening, Mr. Kaplan."

"Please call me Aaron, and yes, it is. But the alternative is to accept ignorance and ugliness as normal, and that's no way to live." Mr. Kaplan's eyes lingered on Mother. "You'll be safe here. If I weren't sure of that, I wouldn't have asked you to stay. I'll see you in the morning."

When the door closed, Grampy looked around at us and said, "I like that man. It don't speak too well for this town that he has to live in fear, does it?"

Grampy told Mother to take the bed. He found a blanket and pillow in the closet, went to a far corner, and bedded down. Within minutes, he was snoring.

Coy went over to Mother and put his arm around her waist. "Mother, it gave me a strange feeling tonight, seeing you dance with a man who wasn't Daddy."

She nodded. "I found it strange too. It happened suddenly. Did you find it good-strange or bad-strange?"

"Well . . . just strange."

"Would you rather I didn't do it again, if the occasion arose?"

He struggled with that. "I guess it would be all right with Mr. Kaplan. Did you know that he loaned *Tom Sawyer* to my brother? Riley McDaniels! He doesn't know Riley very well, does he?"

I gave the twerp a worldly sneer. "Just for that, I'm going to read the first chapter."

"Ha! I'll believe that when I see it."

Coy shared the bed with Mother, and I made a pallet on the floor, near an electric lamp. There, in front of my brother's very eyes, I read the first chapter of *Tom Sawyer.* The next thing I knew, everyone was asleep, and it was two-thirty in the morning.

I had just read six chapters of a book! It was so funny, I couldn't put it down. And Tom Sawyer . . . well, Tom and I had a lot of things in common.

The next morning we were up and moving around when Mr. Kaplan knocked on the door. He came in with a big silver tray with coffee, sweet rolls, and some things I'd never seen before—scrambled eggs and sausage wrapped up in a tortilla. He'd bought them from a Mexican vendor on the street.

After sleeping on the floor all night, Grampy was moaning and hobbling around in his socken feet, but when he caught the smell of black coffee, he came to life. He threw down two cups and gnawed on a sweet roll.

I noticed that he didn't warm up his dentures in Aaron's coffee. He must have known that Mother considered it a nasty habit.

We gathered up our belongings and walked down

to the street. As we were making our way through the store, Aaron asked me if I had started *Tom Sawyer.* I told him, in a voice loud enough for Coy to hear, that I had stayed up until two-thirty and had read six whole chapters.

"Good, excellent. Stay with it."

Then I had the pleasure of seeing the look of surprise on Coy's face. He said, "You did not."

"I certainly did, and I can even tell you what you said in your sleep."

"Uh-uh. What did I say in my sleep?"

"You said, 'Oh Rosie May, I think I love you!'"

Coy scowled and shook his head. "Did not. Riley, you are so . . ."

Mother stepped between us. "Boys, please. Riley, did you actually read six chapters last night?"

"Yes ma'am, I sure did. It's the best book I ever read. I may even finish it."

That pleased her. She put her arm around me and said, "I'm proud of you. Aaron, thank you. You've been a good influence on this one."

It was a bright clear day outside, filled with the sounds of the bustling city—the grinding of motor cars, the blare of horns, the cries of street peddlers, and off in the distance, the ever present hiss of the gas flares and the clanking of the drilling rigs. Once again, we caught the smell of oil and natural gas, mingled now with the more pleasant odors of meat and onions cooking.

Aaron shaded his eyes with a hand and looked out

at the street. "It's an ugly town. There's so little here that pleases the eye. But I admire the spirit of people who come to these boomtowns. It's like the frontier, you know. A year ago it was naked prairie, and now . . . all this. There's an energy about it, a sense of common purpose. Everyone who comes here is looking for a better life, and that makes it very American, doesn't it?

"My parents came from Russia which had many beautiful cities, all built for the glory of the czar. Beautiful cities, palaces, cathedrals, architectural splendors. But who could enjoy them? The spirit of the people had been killed. They knew nothing of the beauty around them, only fear and drudgery. So what is beauty? Perhaps there's a beauty in accomplishment, even in the midst of such noise and squalor."

He noticed that we were all staring at him, and he smiled. "Well, I hope my map will help you find Mrs. Sparrow's house." He shook hands with all of us. "This has been a pleasure."

"For us too, son," said Grampy.

Mother took his hand. "You showed us a side of Sparrow we never would have seen without you. We enjoyed meeting your friends. And you, of course. Thank you."

Aaron smiled. "One day, Sparrow will be a better place. It's worth fighting for. If anything should go wrong with your plans, you're always welcome to stay here. And I hope I'll see you again before you leave town."

We waved good-bye and left Aaron Kaplan with his thoughts.

At ten o'clock in the morning, Sparrow was a blur of noise, movement, people, cars. It all seemed chaotic at first glance, yet like ants, the citizens of Sparrow seemed to be obeying a pattern that wasn't apparent. They were all going somewhere and doing something.

There were probably more people in one block of downtown Sparrow than lived in our entire county. The miracle was not that they sometimes fought and brawled, but that they weren't doing it all the time.

We continued down the street, fascinated by all the strange sights and sounds. A vendor came by, selling pocketknives and can openers. Another was selling cotton work gloves, and another stood on the corner, offering a selection of used boots. A knot of men was singing a hymn in harmony that was as good as anything I'd heard in church, and right beside them stood a well-dressed gentleman selling oil leases. Several women wearing bright silk dresses walked past. Mother eyed them closely but didn't say anything.

In the next block we found ourselves standing in front of The Oasis. The music and laughter pouring out the door were just as rowdy in the morning as they had been the night before. Grampy ran his eyes over the front of the building.

"Would you believe my little sister owns such a wicked place?"

Mother was shocked. "No. Does she?"

"She sure does. It was part of old Uncle George's empire. I think he owned about half the town."

"Well, I hope he's gone to a better place."

We reached the truck and loaded our things into the back. Mother and Coy climbed aboard and I cranked the motor. It was harder than I had remembered, which gave me new respect for Spud Morris's physical strength. He always made it look easy.

The motor kicked over and started, and I hopped into the back end. Mother brought out Aaron Kaplan's map and served as navigator, which was a good thing because Grampy had never been able to read a map.

Ten minutes later, we pulled up in front of a big two-story brick home that sat alone on a hill, surrounded by a well-kept yard, one of the few we had seen in town. Grampy killed the motor and said, "Well, I guess this is the place."

We walked through the wrought-iron gate and up to the door.

Aunt Mattie's house wouldn't have been a showplace in most cities, but in Sparrow, a town of tents, boxy frame buildings, and sheet-iron warehouses, it stood out. It had grass in the yard, flowers blooming in the flower beds, and shrubs that had been planted with some pattern of landscaping.

It faced east, toward the business district, and from the broad porch we could see a forest of wooden derricks in the distance.

"Well," Mother said, "it has a nice view."

Grampy grunted. "It does, if you don't mind seeing

good cow country covered up with junk. I'll wager those old ranchers who leased out their land get sick when they look at all that stuff. It'll take fifty years to get the country back the way it was, if they ever do."

And with that, he knocked on the heavy oak door.

Chapter Fourteen

WE WAITED FOR several minutes. Grampy knocked again. Then the door opened and we found ourselves looking into the cold blue eyes of a tall woman in a nurse's uniform. This was Mrs. Kelly.

She didn't look at all friendly. Her eyes flicked over us, from our feet up to our heads, and then in a flat tone of voice, she said, "Yes?"

Grampy said, "Morning. We're calling for Mattie Sparrow."

"Do you have an appointment?"

"No ma'am, we sure don't. Do we need one?"

"Mrs. Sparrow isn't well. She's not allowed to see visitors."

"We're not visitors. I'm her brother."

"Mrs. Sparrow hasn't mentioned having a brother."

"Well, I *am* her brother, whether she's mentioned it or not."

"I'm sorry. You'll have to come back another time."

She started to close the door but Grampy blocked it with his boot. "Lady, we're coming through that door. The only question is, how much wood do you want to eat?"

This left her speechless for a moment. "All right, come in, but you can't stay long. The doctor said . . ."

Grampy breezed past her. "You send the doctor to me and we'll talk about it."

Mrs. Kelly closed the door, and we entered Aunt Mattie's house. My first impression was that it looked like a museum and smelled like a hospital. It was furnished with expensive antiques and rugs and hanging lamps, and everything was neat and orderly. It had the feel of a place where nobody lived: no magazines or newspapers in sight, no dishes on the tables, no dirt or cobwebs, no coats hanging on pegs, no shoes lying around. It was a little bit eerie.

Mrs. Kelly moved past us, the heels of her shoes echoing down the hallway. "Follow me."

We moved past a stairway that led to the upstairs, with hardwood bannisters on both sides, through a large dining room, and on to the rear of the house. There, Mrs. Kelly came to a closed door. She stood for a moment, listening, then turned the knob and swung it open. She motioned for us to come. When Grampy approached, she whispered, "I repeat: she's very ill."

Grampy scowled at her. "Honey, why don't you wait outside? If we need you, we'll holler."

"The doctor won't like this."

"Time heals all wounds."

Shaking her head and moving her lips, Mrs. Kelly left the room, and we all turned to the bed. It was a large bed with four sculpted wooden posters, and in the middle of it lay a tiny woman. The cover was pulled neatly to her chest and her hands lay on top. Her face was ghostly pale and her lips seemed almost blue.

When Mother saw Aunt Mattie, her breath caught in her throat.

Grampy went over and sat on the edge of the bed. Mother said, "Daddy, you shouldn't sit on the bed. That nurse will howl if she comes back in and finds you."

"Let 'er howl. It might liven up this place a little bit." He took one of Mattie's hands and gave it a pat. "Mattie? Can you hear me?" There was no sign of life, yet we could see that she was breathing. "Mattie, you've got company. See if you can crack open your eyes for just a minute."

Her eyelids quivered, then slid open, revealing a pair of eyes that were as blue as a summer sky. She looked at the ceiling for a minute, then her gaze drifted over our faces.

In a distant whisper, she said, "Who are you?" Then her eyes settled on Grampy. "Abner? Is that you?"

"Well, it's what's left of me after sixty hard years."

She stared at him, then her lip began to quiver, as though she were about to cry. He patted her hand and told her to lie still, but she shook her head and struggled. She leaned toward him and whispered, "DON'T. LEAVE. ME."

Those three words hung in the silence of the house as Aunt Mattie closed her eyes and her head fell back on the pillow. Mother and Grampy exchanged long worried looks, then Mother said, "Daddy, what did she mean by that?"

Grampy shook his head. "I don't know, but I heard what she said. From now on, one of us will stay in this room at all times."

Mother nodded.

Just then, we heard footsteps outside the room. There was a tap at the door. Mother motioned for me to open it, and when the door swung open, we found ourselves looking into the cold blue eyes of Nurse Kelly. Behind her stood a man in a suit. In his right hand he held a black bowler hat, and in his left hand was a black bag. His head was almost bald and he looked at us with suspicious eyes.

The nurse's gaze went first to Aunt Mattie, then to Grampy. "The doctor is here. Sir, you shouldn't be sitting on the bed."

She stepped aside and the doctor entered the

room. Grampy rose and offered his hand. "I'm Abner Dawson, Mattie's brother."

The doctor shook his hand. "I'm Dr. Wallace, her physician. George and I were close friends. Mattie told me she had a brother. I'm glad you're here." Grampy introduced the rest of us to Dr. Wallace. He gave us each a cordial greeting, then his face grew serious. "As you can see, your sister isn't doing well."

"Yes, we noticed that, and could we discuss it?" Grampy made eye motions toward the nurse, who was now smoothing out Aunt Mattie's covers, where Grampy had left some wrinkles.

Dr. Wallace cleared his throat. "Mrs. Kelly, I'd like a few moments alone with the family."

"Certainly," she said, and left the room without looking at us.

When the door closed, Grampy turned to the doctor. "Who is that hateful old bat, and what does she do around here? I've stepped on rattlesnakes that had more charm than she's got."

Dr. Wallace smiled. "Mrs. Kelly was the best nurse in Amarillo. I hired her myself."

"I feel sorry for her husband." Grampy turned to Mother. "Don't you know he looks forward to seeing her at night? I'd sooner face a bitin' dog."

Mother scowled and said, "Daddy . . . shhh."

Dr. Wallace went on. "She's a widow, Mr. Dawson, and I'll grant that she lacks social graces, but that's not uncommon in nurses. Oftentimes the best ones aren't very pleasant."

Grampy nodded. "Well, that sure fits."

"But with Mrs. Kelly, your sister is getting the best of care. I promise you that."

"Uh-huh. Well, my first thought is that just being in the same house with her would make most people sick, but let's skip that for now. Tell us about Mattie."

The doctor furrowed his brow. "It was strange how this came on her. She was strong and vigorous through George's last illness. He had a heart condition, you may know, and he was bedridden for several days. Mattie stayed at his side day and night, and seemed a tower of strength. At the funeral she grieved, as you would expect, but it was nothing out of the ordinary.

"But the very next day I began to see signs of a decline. I was here with her, going over some matters dealing with George's estate, and I noticed that she seemed . . . distracted. Her mind seemed to wander. She couldn't concentrate on the details of George's business. Decisions had to be made and finally I asked if she wanted me to take care of the business until she had some time to recover. She seemed grateful and relieved, and said that, yes, she would certainly appreciate my lending a hand.

"I sent her straight to bed, gave her some medicine to calm her nerves, and engaged Mrs. Kelly to look after her day and night, and also to keep the house. I had no reason to suspect that Mattie wouldn't recover after a few days' sleep. Usually that's all it takes, you know. The shock of losing a loved one, the ordeal of the funeral . . . it takes its toll, even on those who have a strong constitution."

He walked over to the window and looked out. "But with Mattie, it wasn't that way. She seemed to grow weaker and more remote. She didn't respond to visitors. The medicine didn't seem to help. We buried George four weeks ago, and Mattie has gotten weaker by the day."

Grampy nodded. "What's wrong with her?"

The doctor turned suddenly and faced us. "I hate to say this, Mr. Dawson, but it's almost as though she has lost her will to live, as though . . . she wants to join George. They were deeply devoted to each other, I'm sure you knew that."

Grampy said, "Can't say that I knew that, no."

"Oh yes, I knew them both quite well, especially George. I was his physician but also a friend and busi-ness associate. We played poker together and shared some investments. I advised him on business matters. George made some shrewd investments, but he wasn't a good manager. Once he'd turned a deal, he tended to lose interest in the details, and that made him vulnerable to fast-talkers and promoters. Sparrow is full of those people, you know."

Grampy nodded. "So we've heard. Doc, why would Mattie sign a piece of paper to force her niece off the ranch?"

"The eviction notice?" Dr. Wallace frowned. "I wondered about that myself. It was Mattie's idea. I as-sumed she wanted to sell the ranch."

"But why didn't she tell my daughter? If she wanted to sell the place, all she needed to do was say so. It seems fishy to me."

The doctor shrugged. "They say you never really know a person until there's some money involved. How long will you be in town?"

Mother and Grampy traded glances, and Grampy said, "We're not sure about that. Let's just say that we've got no plans to leave in a hurry. In fact . . ." He hitched up his pants. ". . . we need to talk about that. We're going to stay here in the house, and one of us is going to be in this room all the time."

The doctor seemed surprised. "Well, I really don't think . . . Mrs. Kelly might not approve of that, Mr. Dawson."

"Uh-huh. Well, Mrs. Kelly is liable to have a bad week, 'cause a lot of things are fixing to change and she ain't going to like any of 'em. I guess if things get unbearable, she can always go outside and trim the bushes. Or draw her wages."

Dr. Wallace managed a smile. "We don't want that, do we? She's a trained nurse and your sister needs the care. But I'm glad you're going to stay a while. It's always good to have family close by. I'll feel better knowing that you're here."

He went over to the bed and checked Aunt Mattie's pulse. He gave his head a shake. "Still very weak. It's important that she continue taking her medicine. I'll check her again this afternoon. I suppose you can handle things with Mrs. Kelly. If you need me, there's a telephone in the hallway." He nodded to Mother. "It was nice meeting you, Mrs. McDaniels. If Mattie were herself, she'd be glad to have you in her home."

He went out and closed the door behind him. We could hear him and Mrs. Kelly speaking out in the hall in low voices.

Mother turned to Grampy. "What do you think, Daddy?"

He rubbed the stubble of whiskers on his cheek and stared at the floor. "Well, he seems a nice feller. There's just one little thing that bothers me—him talking about Mattie and George being so devoted to each other, and her wanting to drift on up to heaven to be with old George. Somehow that don't sound right."

Mother nodded. "Now that you mention it, it doesn't sound right. They weren't exactly lovebirds."

"She was an old maid who needed a husband, and he was an old codger who needed a wife. Getting married was handy for both of 'em, and it worked out nice." Grampy's eyes drifted over to the bed. "But as far as her grieving herself to death . . ."

There was a knock at the door, and Mrs. Kelly walked in. She held a medicine bottle in one hand and a spoon in the other. "It's time for Mrs. Sparrow's medicine."

She went to the bed, lifted Aunt Mattie's head, and gave her a spoonful of medicine. Aunt Mattie didn't open her eyes and her lips moved weakly, but she managed to swallow most of it. Mrs. Kelly wiped Aunt Mattie's mouth and eased her head back on the pillow.

Then she turned to Grampy. "Dr. Wallace said you plan to stay here in the house."

Grampy twirled his hat around on his finger. "Yes, that's right."

She stiffened and cut her eyes at me and Coy. "Really, Mr. Dawson, I don't think your sister needs the noise of children in the house. The doctor was too polite to say anything, but I hope you understand . . . this is *not* a good idea."

Grampy kept twirling his hat. "You know, nurse, when me and you first laid eyes on each other, I had a feeling that we weren't going to be great friends. But I think that after we've gotten better acquainted, we'll like each other even less." Mrs. Kelly's nostrils flared and she started out of the room. "Oh, and you can leave that medicine. My daughter'll take care of it."

She thrust the bottle and spoon out to Mother. "One tablespoon every three hours." She left the room.

Grampy watched her leave. "I've got a bad feeling about that nurse." He took the bottle from Mother, opened it up, and sniffed it. Then he put some on his tongue. He made a sour face. "Must be good medicine. It tastes like it was made by Satan himself."

Chapter Fifteen

FOR THE REST of the day, Mother and Grampy took turns sitting beside Aunt Mattie's bed, and every three hours, they gave her the medicine. Dr. Wallace came in the late afternoon, took Aunt Mattie's pulse, and left without saying much, only that she didn't seem to be better or worse.

Coy burrowed into his book and didn't seem to mind the waiting, and Grampy took several naps. I thought I would go crazy, listening to the ticking of the grandfather clock in the living room. I paced the room and gazed out the windows, until Mother finally told me to sit down and read *Tom Sawyer*. For some reason, I hadn't thought of that. Sure enough, it helped pass the time. For the next two hours, I was fishing on the Mississippi River with Huck and Tom.

Around six, Mrs. Kelly came to the door and told Mother that she had fixed us some chicken soup for supper. That was our first indication that Mrs. Kelly might be something other than a dragon. She seemed to have accepted our presence in the house, although I noticed that there was still ice between her and Grampy. They eyed each other in the manner of cats and dogs.

The meal was a very solemn affair. We sat at the long dinner table and nobody talked. Every clank of a spoon, every tick of the clock was amplified by the silence. At last, Grampy laid down his spoon.

"Nurse, did you put any meat in this soup, or did you just let the chicken walk around in the water?"

Coy and I could hardly keep from laughing out loud, but Mother wasn't amused. "Daddy, that's rude."

"Well, sugar, I've spent the last five minutes searching for a piece of meat."

Mother told him to hush, and she apologized to Mrs. Kelly. "This waiting around is getting on everyone's nerves."

Mrs. Kelly said she understood, but she and Grampy continued to bristle every time they shared the same space.

At bedtime, Grampy told Mother to go on to bed and he would stay in the room with Aunt Mattie, but Mother said she would take the first watch. Mrs. Kelly brought her some quilts and blankets from the linen closet, and made a pallet on the floor.

Around ten o'clock, I happened to pass by the darkened living room and heard fiddle music. I tiptoed into the room and saw Grampy, sitting in front of a big console radio. His face was lighted by the glow of the radio tubes in the dark. The music stopped and the announcer's voice came on:

"Thank you, boys, thank you so much. And that brings us to the end of another show with the Light Crust Dough Boys and their sweet country music. Tune in again next week on WBAP for more of the same."

Grampy leaned forward and snapped off the radio. He sat there for a moment, staring off into space. Then he looked up and saw me.

"Oh. I didn't hear you."

"Is that Mr. Wills's band?" Grampy nodded. "They're good."

"They're real good. That Wills kid has a special flare. I knew it the first time I heard him play."

"I'm sorry you're not playing with them. But Grampy, I'm sure glad you're here."

He stood up, stretched, and patted me on the shoulder. "Well, son, a man has to tend to the important things first. The rest will take care of itself. It's taken me quite a while to learn that. Now let's get some sleep."

Dr. Wallace stopped by the next morning around ten. He took Aunt Mattie's pulse and shook his head. "Mr. Dawson, I have to tell you that this could go on for quite a while. I don't know how long you planned to stay, but . . ."

Mother said, "Do you suppose we could take her back to the ranch with us?"

"I wouldn't advise that. She's better off here, in her own house and her own bed."

Grampy scowled. "Well, so far it don't seem to be doing her a whole lot of good."

The doctor nodded. "No, but as weak as she is, a long trip could be very bad. I'm sorry. I wish I could do more."

The waiting began again. The clock ticked and we read our books. Then, around three in the afternoon, the telephone rang. Mrs. Kelly answered it and said, "It's for Riley McDaniels." Everyone stared at me. Who could be calling me? I had never spoken on a telephone before.

Aaron Kaplan's voice was on the other end. "Riley, hello. How is life at the Sparrow mansion?"

"It's pretty quiet. I'm sure glad I have a good book to read."

"Yes, indeed. Well, did you know that Lindbergh landed in Paris this morning?"

"No sir. Who's Lindbergh?"

"Charles Lindbergh. He flew *The Spirit of Saint Louis* nonstop from New York to Paris. The newspapers have been full of it for days, and that's all you hear on the radio. Don't tell me you didn't know about it."

"Mr. Kaplan, where we live, nobody has ever heard of Charles Lindbergh. We've just recently heard about Paris."

He laughed. "Well, I wish you could see down-town. I've never seen anything like it. People are going around hugging each other, and everyone is talking about Lindbergh, Lindbergh! Actually, I called to see if you boys would like to take a drive out into the country. I know you must be getting tired of sitting around. They're bringing in an oil well north of town and there's talk that it might be a gusher. That would be something to see. What do you say?"

"I'd love it! But I'd better ask Mother."

"Of course. She's welcome to come too, and Abner as well."

"Okay, hang on. I'll go ask."

I ran back into Aunt Mattie's room. They were all anxious to know who had called, and I told them that Mr. Kaplan had invited us to go for a ride. Mother said, "How thoughtful of him. You boys go, and you too, Daddy. I'll stay here with Aunt Mattie."

Grampy thought for a moment and shook his head. "No, you were with her all last night. You need a break. This sitting around is hard."

"Well, it's hard on you too."

He showed her the palm of his hand. "I'll be fine. Y'all go. Who knows, me and that nurse might strike up a game of horseshoes while you're gone."

I ran back to the phone. "Mr. Kaplan? Sure, we can go."

"I'll be there in ten minutes."

Coy and I were watching at the front window when we saw a fancy blue Chevrolet sedan stop in front of the house.

Aaron had started toward the house and met us at the gate. He was wearing a black brimmed hat and a vested suit, and looked very dapper. He greeted us with a smile and opened the car door for Mother. It was a four-door automobile, and Coy and I climbed into the back. Inside, we glanced around and Coy said, "Wow, this is a beautiful car! Is it new?"

We pulled away and Aaron said, "You like it? Yes, I bought it a month ago. I like the color, don't you? Chevrolet is offering several colors now in addition to black. They're putting pressure on Ford, and I've heard that old Henry is going to respond by bringing out an entirely new car—not a modified Model T, but a new car. It's still under wraps but they're leaking little tidbits to the newspapers. It's going to be called the Model A and they're going to offer it in several colors." He looked at Mother. "Do cars interest you?"

"If we could afford one like this, they would interest me a lot. It's very nice, and I love the material on these seats."

"Do you drive?"

"Oh yes." She paused for a moment. "I drive a team and wagon."

He laughed. "You don't have an automobile?"

"No. My late husband was planning to buy one eventually but . . ." She looked out the window. "Out where we live, a car wouldn't do well. Our roads are rough and the mud can be terrible. Daddy has that old truck, but we still depend on our horses to get us around."

"So . . . do you ride? In a saddle?"

She nodded. "I'm a ranch woman. I do whatever has to be done. Some days I'm a mother, some days I'm feeding cattle out of a wagon, some days I put on pants and ride horseback with my boys. That must sound drab to a man like you."

"Oh, not at all. I've always been fascinated by the . . . what do we call it? The mystique of the cowboy? When I moved to Texas, I thought I would be surrounded by cowboys, but . . . well, Sparrow is an industrial town. It's no more cowboy than Pittsburgh. So you ride and do . . . cowboy work?"

She nodded. "When we get back to the ranch, we'll start our branding work. We'll all be on horseback for that."

Coy said, "It's fun, Mr. Kaplan. You should come. Do you have any kids?"

Mother scolded Coy for being nosy, but Aaron didn't seem to mind. "No, Coy, I've never had the pleasure of being married. My business seems to take me to places where there isn't an abundance of ladies. But I'd love to come to your branding."

Mother studied his profile for a moment, then said, "If you have a pencil and paper, I'll draw you a map to the ranch."

Aaron found a parking place on Main Street and pulled into it. He rummaged through the glove box until he found a clean sheet of paper and a pencil. He gave them to Mother.

While Mother worked on the map, Aaron walked

across the street and went into an ice-cream parlor. When he came out, he was carrying two ice-cream cones, but his face seemed troubled. He handed us the cones through the window and said, "Boys, I hope this isn't a mistake. Try to keep the ice cream off the seats."

He got into the car and pulled out into the street. Coy and I licked the drips on our ice cream, which had begun to melt in the heat of the afternoon. As we gained speed, I noticed that Mother was watching Aaron.

"Aaron, is something wrong?"

"No, no, it's nothing." He gave her a smile and turned his eyes back to the road.

Mother was silent for a moment. "You were different when you came out of the ice-cream store."

"Really? You're a keen observer."

Mother waited.

"All right, there was something. As I was leaving the store, the owner, whom I know slightly, said 'Mr. Kaplan, be careful.' I don't know why he would say that. I'm sure it was nothing."

Chapter Sixteen

WE MADE OUR way through the busy streets and drove out of town to the north. Coy and I lapped our ice cream and Mother looked out the window. Then she said, "I would be concerned if someone had said that to me. Is there some particular reason why you should be careful?"

"Not that I know of. Well, all of us in the reform group live with a certain amount of . . . let's call it tension. We know they're watching us, but so far they haven't made our lives unbearable. After all, they're extorting money from us every week. If they run us out of town, who will fill their coffers? It's a game of cat and mouse. They follow us, we elude them. They bluster and we ignore, and every week Constable McGreggor comes around and collects his ten dollars. Please, don't give it another thought."

Mother smiled. I knew that smile. It meant that she would let the subject drop for now, and she would give it *plenty* of thought. For the rest of the day, she would be watching everyone and everything.

Aaron pointed to some tents that were sprawled out on a mesquite flat east of the road. "It's called Ragtown. Everyone there lives in tents because there's such a shortage of housing. I hope they'll have better places to live before winter."

As we drove by, six barefoot children stopped playing and stared at us. I caught a glimpse of one of them, a boy who might have been eleven or twelve years old, Coy's age. He had been rolling an old tire. His face was dirty and his red hair stuck up in the back. The cuffs of his striped overalls struck him two inches above the ankles. When we passed, he raised his right hand in a solemn greeting.

Mother said, "I can't imagine trying to raise a family in a tent. I don't know how those women do it."

"They're able to do it," said Aaron, "because, believe it or not, they're here to escape something even worse."

Mother shivered and said to me and Coy, "Boys, don't ever forget to count your blessings. We have much to be thankful for."

Several miles north of town, we came to a steep hill

that took us down into the Canadian River valley. Aaron geared the car down so that the motor helped slow our descent, and we made our way down to the bottom. There, we turned onto a two-rut trail that led into a pasture that was dotted with scrubby mesquite trees. We came to a wooden derrick which was identified by a sign as Tidwell #2.

Aaron parked in a line of thirty or forty automobiles. "Here we are. I think we made it in time. It doesn't appear that the well has blown in yet. We can get out, but watch where you step. There's a lot of oil and grease around these locations."

Aaron opened Mother's door. As she stepped out of the car, she handed Aaron the map she had drawn. "We'll let you know when we set a date for the branding."

"Oh, thank you." Aaron looked at the map, then folded it up and slipped it into the inside pocket of his jacket. "You draw a good map."

"Thank you." Mother stood beside the car for a moment, looking off in the distance. "Aaron, if you should ever need a place of refuge, you'd be welcome to stay with us."

Aaron stared at her and then laughed. "Refuge? I don't think it's that bad, not yet. But thank you for the offer."

Mother smiled.

We drifted over to a crowd of people who were standing in the shadow of the huge wooden derrick. I was surprised to see that most of them were dressed up, the men in white shirts and ties, and several women wearing long dresses and straw hats.

I asked Aaron why they had worn their best clothes to an event which would feature a well spewing mud and crude oil in all directions. He shrugged and said, "It's a social occasion. In Sparrow we have no opera, symphony orchestra, or theater, so we dress up to watch a well blow in. It seems a bit silly, doesn't it? But we make the best out of what we have. And besides, every new well is good for business."

Shading our eyes, we waited and watched the mud-spattered men working around the derrick, and listened to the hiss and bang of the steam engine that pounded the drilling tool deeper and deeper into the earth. All at once, we heard shouting from the derrick, and the workers began running in all directions. Then came a low rumble from the ground, and a geyser of oil and mud spewed out of the hole and went high in the air. A cheer rose from the crowd, as all eyes followed the spray of oil in the sky.

In the midst of the excitement, I noticed that a man came over to Aaron and whispered something in his ear. I recognized him: Bernie Marks, the locksmith. Aaron's expression darkened. He took Mother by the arm and said, "I'm sorry, but we have to leave." They walked briskly toward the car, and Coy and I fell in behind them, regretting that we couldn't stay and watch the gusher a little longer.

As we pulled away from the location, Aaron's eyes and lips were tight, and we could all feel tension in the air. He turned left onto the main road and we started up the long hill back to town.

At last Mother said, "Aaron, what is it?"

He didn't look at her. "I'm not sure. Something about my store." He glanced in his rearview mirror. "Also, I think we're being followed."

Mother, Coy, and I turned around and looked behind us where, some four hundred yards to the north, there was a black coupe. Mother said, "What makes you think he's following us?"

"Just a feeling, but we can find out for sure."

Suddenly he stopped in the middle of the big hill and began coasting backward. The car behind us drew closer. Aaron swung the wheel to the left, turned completely around so that we were now heading north, and down the hill we went, passing the black Ford. Aaron waved as we passed the two startled men inside, then he turned his eyes to the rearview mirror.

"As I thought. They're following us."

Mother gave him a troubled look. "Who are they?"

"I'm not sure. Some of the local riffraff. They've never done this before."

Sure enough, the black car had turned around and was behind us again. Aaron sped up and turned left on the next dirt road he came to, which twisted up a hill in a westerly direction. "We can get back to town this way," he murmured. "Well! Apparently I made a mistake in asking you good people to share my day. This isn't what I had in mind. I apologize for exposing you to my difficulties, and perhaps even to some danger. To tell you the truth, Sara . . . may I call you that?"

"Of course you may."

"Thank you. To tell you the truth, I have no idea why they're following me. I assume it's just harassment."

"What did that man tell you?"

Aaron glanced into the mirror. "Bernie heard a rumor that the police are planning to close up my store, on the pretext that it's a fire hazard or something like that."

"And they can do that?"

"Of course they can. The whiskey ring has bought the police and enough judges to have their own way. The rest of us operate at their whim. It's an intolerable situation, and it may be coming to a head. Soon." Aaron's car climbed the hill in low gear. When we reached the top of the caprock and broke out onto the flats, he looked back at Coy and me. "The salesman said this Chevrolet was the fastest car on the road. Let's see."

He slipped the car into high gear and gave it the gas. Coy and I watched out the back window and reported that we were pulling away from the pursuers. At the base of a small hill, Aaron turned east onto an oil field road and we took back roads into town. We saw no more of the black Ford, and this seemed to raise Aaron's spirits. He laughed and joked the rest of the way into town.

But when we arrived in front of his store, his eyes turned grim again. Someone had stretched a rope around the front of his store and attached several red flags to it, and a policeman was slouched against one of the porch posts. He wore a pistol and was twirling a wooden billy club.

We parked at the curb and Aaron got out. "Wait here. I don't want you involved in this. I'll see what it's all about." He walked over to the officer. "This is my store. What is the problem?"

"Fire marshal's orders. You've got a coal stove in there."

"Of course I have a coal stove. What other kind of stove would I have?"

The officer shrugged. "Coal's dangerous. It burns."

"Yes, it does, which is one of the reasons it's popular as a fuel for heating. What would you have me burn in my stove? Rocks?"

"Fire marshal says it's dangerous."

Just then, a big man wearing a suit and bowler hat came walking up. It was Constable McGreggor. He gave Aaron a smirk. "Sure sorry to hear about the store getting closed."

In a bitter voice Aaron said, "If you're so sorry, don't close it. I've done nothing wrong, and this talk about a fire hazard is nonsense."

The constable cracked a peanut and popped the nuts into his mouth. "You know, Mr. Kaplan, the talk around town is that you're a dangerous radical. Is there any truth to that?"

"I sell clothes, Constable, and I pay the police to leave me alone."

The constable's smile faded. "I'll pretend I didn't hear that. Now, you run along, Mr. Kaplan, and I'd advise you and your friends . . ."

He dropped his voice and we didn't hear the rest.

When Aaron returned to the car, his face was tight with anger. We roared away from the store.

"They're going to try to choke the life out of us," Aaron said. "Well, we'll see about that. Tonight, we make our move. We'll telegraph our petition to the governor with the names of twenty-five citizens and merchants, and then we'll let these scum deal with the Texas Rangers."

Mother stared at him. "The Texas Rangers!"

"It's our only hope. We didn't want it to come to this, but we have no choice. We can't break their grip on the town without help from the outside."

He drove us back to Aunt Mattie's house and parked out front. He had calmed down a little. "I neglected to ask about your aunt. How is she doing?"

"Gravely ill," said Mother. "She regained consciousness just long enough to recognize Daddy and to tell him not to leave. I don't understand why she said that."

"What does Dr. Frankel say? I assume she's under Dr. Frankel's care." Mother shook her head. Aaron frowned. "Sara, he's the only competent doctor in town. Who's taking care of her?" When Mother told him Dr. Wallace, Aaron stared at her. "Ben Wallace?"

"Yes. He's a longtime friend of the family, and he seems a nice man. What is it?"

"Oh, nothing. This is none of my business."

"Aaron!"

Aaron took a deep breath and drummed his fingers on the steering wheel. "I don't know the man personally, so I could be wrong . . . look, he calls himself Dr. Wallace, and maybe he really was a doctor at one time, but around this town, it's a kind of joke."

"A joke?"

"Let me try to explain this. Prohibition is very unpopular, not just here in Sparrow but all over the nation. One way of getting around the law is to sell liquor as though it were medicine, so in many towns, there's some character who calls himself Dr. So-and-so and his main practice consists of prescribing whiskey."

Mother stared at him. "Ben Wallace does that? He's not actually a doctor?"

"I can't say that for sure, but I can tell you that he has a shady reputation. If someone in my family were sick, I wouldn't want Ben Wallace as the physician."

"But he was Uncle George's friend and business partner. Surely . . ."

Mother's voice trailed off into silence. Aaron pressed his lips together and said, "I can do some research on this. I have contacts in Austin. In the meantime, let me talk to Dr. Frankel. Maybe he should examine Mrs. Sparrow. Would that be all right?"

Mother's head slumped against the window. "Yes. Please."

As we got out of the car, Aaron spoke to Mother. "I'll give some thought to what you said about a refuge. And I won't lose the map."

Chapter Seventeen

WE WATCHED AARON drive off, then went into the house—the big echoing house that smelled like a hospital and felt like a museum, where time was marked by the ticking of the grandfather clock, and a frail old woman struggled to stay alive.

That house gave me the shivers, and I didn't look forward to spending another night in it.

We found Grampy napping in a chair beside Aunt Mattie's bed, and it appeared that she hadn't moved one bit in the time we had been gone. Grampy grumbled about his stiff neck and asked us about our trip.

Mother told him what Aaron had said about Ben

Wallace. "Daddy, I don't understand what's going on around here, but something's wrong."

Grampy got up and paced around the room. "Honey, I've thought something was wrong since the minute we got here, only I thought it was the nurse."

Aaron called an hour later and told Mother what he'd learned from his contacts in Austin. Ben Wallace had attended two years of medical school and dropped out. He had practiced medicine without a license in several Texas towns, and had been exposed on two occasions. In 1924 he was accused of looting the assets of a bank in Decatur, Texas, though the case against him was never proved.

Mother gave us this report, then said, "Aunt Mattie probably didn't know any of this, the poor thing. She thought Ben Wallace was a doctor and trusted him."

Dr. Frankel came as soon as he could, looking as dapper as ever in his blue suit, but wearing a grim expression that matched the way we were all feeling. He gave us a nod and went straight to Aunt Mattie. He listened to her heartbeat, took her pulse, and examined her fingernails. Then he said, "Let me see the medicine."

Mother handed him the bottle. He smelled it, then put a dab of it on his finger and tasted it. His shaggy eyebrows rose as he turned to Grampy. "Mr. Dawson, I don't know what's going on here, but my opinion is that this is a mild solution of arsenic."

"Arsenic! You mean poison?"

"Yes sir. It accumulates in the system over time, and then it's fatal."

All at once Grampy cocked his head, raised one finger to his lips, and began creeping over to the door. He reached out and wrapped his hand around the doorknob. He turned the knob and jerked at the same time . . . and Nurse Kelly came stumbling into the room.

She had been leaning with her ear against the door, eavesdropping on our conversation.

Grampy said, "Well, nurse, won't you come in? We've got a few questions for you."

Mrs. Kelly glanced over at Mother. "I apologize, Mrs. McDaniels. I'm not a snoop, but there's something very, very wrong in this house and I don't know what it is. I don't know whom to trust."

Grampy snorted a laugh. "Well, thunder, I can set you straight on that. There ain't but ten people in this whole town worth trusting, and five of 'em are here in this room. It's you I'm wondering about."

Her eyes narrowed in anger. "What do you have against me? You've hated me from the moment you first saw me."

"No. I've hated you from the moment you tried to slam my foot in the door. Before that, it was just a heavy dislike."

"I've done my best to care for your sister!" she yelled, almost in tears. "The doctor told me not to admit visitors. You came crashing in here like a . . . like a buffalo! What was I supposed to do?"

Grampy glared at her. "Nurse, Ben Wallace isn't a doctor, and you've been giving my sister arsenic."

Mrs. Kelly stared at him in disbelief. "What? Oh my heavens, I've been poisoning the poor woman!" She buried her face in her hands and started crying. Mother went over and comforted her. "How could I have been so stupid! I knew something was wrong. She never got better, only worse—every hour, every day, just worse! I should have trusted my instincts."

Mother turned to Grampy. "Daddy, what on earth is going on around here?"

Grampy's eyebrows rose and fell. "Well, Sara, I'm guessing that Ben Wallace has sunk his hooks into Mattie's business affairs. He got her doped up and had her sign that eviction notice, and who knows what else. Now he's waiting for her to croak. And if we don't get her out of here . . ."

Just then, I heard a car pull up in front of the house. I ran to the window and peeked out. "It's him! It's Ben Wallace!"

It was then that I remembered where I'd heard that name before: in the car with Aunt Mattie and Uncle George, after the funeral. Uncle George had said, "I think he's gone crooked."

Grampy turned to Mrs. Kelly. "Nurse, you've got to get hold of yourself. Take that medicine bottle. Pour the stuff out and refill it with something brown. Coffee. We don't want Wallace getting suspicious, not just yet."

Mrs. Kelly took the medicine bottle and hurried out.

Grampy turned to Dr. Frankel. "Doc, you'd better get out of here. Use the back door."

Dr. Frankel started out, shaking his head. "You heard about Aaron? They've closed his store. It's all coming to a head. Our group meets tonight. Oh, this is terrible, terrible!"

"Doc, we need to get my sister out of here. Is it safe to move her?"

The doctor was silent for a moment. "Her system needs time to recover. Twenty-four hours. Come to my office tomorrow at noon and we'll talk."

Dr. Frankel hurried out, just as Ben Wallace knocked on the front door and entered the house.

A tense silence moved over us. We waited. At last, Nurse Kelly swept into the room and set the bottle down on a table beside the bed. We all heaved a sigh of relief.

We heard Wallace's footsteps outside in the hallway. In a low voice Grampy said, "Nurse, let's me and you provide a little scene here." She nodded that she understood. Grampy spoke to her in a loud voice. "Well, you might call that stuff food, Mrs. Kelly, but I'd call it something else! That fried steak of yours ain't fit for hogs!"

Mrs. Kelly got into character and shrieked, "Well, that's fine, you ungrateful, ill-tempered old lizard! If you don't like my cooking, you can just make your own!"

"Well, don't think I can't, sweetheart. I've eaten boiled owl that tasted better than what you call fried steak."

Ben Wallace walked in. "Excuse me. Am I interrupting something?"

Mrs. Kelly shot a finger toward Grampy. "That man is impossible!" She put her nose in the air and went clacking out of the room, slamming the door behind her.

Mr. Wallace ran his gaze around the room. "What was that all about?"

Grampy looked up at the ceiling. "Oh, we were just discussing her talents as a chef. We'd decided she don't have any, and I think it made her mad."

Mr. Wallace nodded. "I got that impression. But don't forget, Mr. Dawson, she's a nurse, not a chef."

"I'm aware of that—every time I take a bite of that slop she puts out. I'm not sure I can stand it much longer."

Mr. Wallace fingered the stethoscope for a moment. "Maybe it would be better for everyone if you went back home for a while."

Grampy's eyes moved into a cunning squint. "You know, Doc, I was just thinking the same thing myself. I can't stand this sitting around all day. And there's something else. This town kind of makes me uneasy." He lowered his voice. "Doc, did you know they sell *whiskey* here? Why, that's against the law."

Wallace stared at him for a moment, then broke out into a laugh. "This is a boomtown, Mr. Dawson.

Our laws are a little different." He went over to the bed. "Well, how's the patient?"

Mother said, "I was about to give her the medicine."

"Good." He put on his stethoscope and listened to Aunt Mattie's heart. "Any change today?"

Mother shook her head. "None."

Wallace nodded and looked up at Grampy. "So . . . you think you'll be leaving?"

"I think so. We'll stay maybe another day or two, then get along home. I can't see that we're doing Mattie much good staying here."

"No, it seems to be a waiting game. She'll either get better or worse. Mrs. Kelly can handle things here, and I'll let you know if there's a change." He turned to Mother. "The medicine?"

Mother jumped up and gave Aunt Mattie the "medicine." Mr. Wallace watched and seemed satisfied. Then he walked to the door. "I'll be back in the morning."

He said good-bye and left. None of us said a word. Coy went over and sat in Mother's lap. Grampy eased over to the window and peeked through the curtain. When the car pulled away from the house, Mrs. Kelly came into the room. "Who is that man?"

"Well, he's a crook . . . a crook in a town full of crooks. Mrs. Kelly, I was wrong about you. I'm sorry. Your fried steak was better than boiled owl."

She smiled. "Thank you. You're not an old lizard."

"Mrs. Kelly, we've got to stay here one more day.

Nobody would blame you if you wanted to leave, but we'd sure appreciate it if you'd stay."

Mrs. Kelly pressed her lips together and nodded. "I'll stay."

The next twenty-four hours were almost unbearable. It had been bad enough before we'd known the truth about "Doctor" Wallace, but now that we knew, we had to live with fear as well as the tedium of waiting.

In the dreadful silence of the house, the clock ticked and Grampy paced like a coyote in a cage. Mother and Mrs. Kelly took turns sitting beside Aunt Mattie's bed, waiting for some signs of improvement. Several times she groaned and called out in her sleep, but that was all.

Coy and I occupied ourselves by reading our books, playing outside in the yard, and helping Mrs. Kelly with some of the household chores. The only bright spot of the day came at seven o'clock that evening, when I snapped my book shut and announced to Mother that I had finished *Tom Sawyer.*

The next morning, Friday, Coy, Grampy, and I left the house and walked into town. I was never so glad to be leaving a place. Aunt Mattie's mansion had begun to remind me of a prison, and I couldn't wait to go home. Grampy and Coy felt the same way.

On our way to Dr. Frankel's office, we made our way down the boardwalk, which was just as noisy and clogged with people as it had been the day we'd arrived. As we passed in front of The Oasis, two rowdy men came out the door, laughing about some adventure in the oil field. They bumped into me, and knocked me off the boardwalk and into the street. They yelled an apology and went on their way.

As I lay in the street, my eyes happened to go to a window on the second floor of The Oasis. Just for an instant, I caught a glimpse of a man in the window. He seemed to be . . . gesturing at me. Puzzled, I waved back. And then he was gone.

Grampy stepped off the boardwalk and offered me his hand. "People in this town could use a few lessons in manners."

"Grampy, I saw a man's face in that window. Just for a second, I thought . . ."

"Thought what?"

"Oh, nothing."

We resumed our walk to Dr. Frankel's office, a small wooden building just off of Main Street. Beside the door hung a sign which read A. FRANKEL, M.D. Inside, we took our seats in the waiting room, joining a man who was suffering with a bad tooth and another whose hand was wrapped in a dirty, bloody rag. After a bit, the door to the examining room opened, and Dr. Frankel escorted a patient out. The doctor was about to call to one of the other men, when he saw us. He crooked his finger at Grampy, telling us to follow him inside.

He closed the door behind him, turned to us with a very solemn expression on his face, and in a low voice said, "Have you heard the news?" Grampy shook his head. "Aaron's disappeared. Our group met last night and we telegraphed our petition to the governor. Aaron was supposed to spend the night at my house. We agreed it might not be safe for him to go back to the store. I waited up and he never came."

Grampy said, "Well, maybe he found another place to stay."

Dr. Frankel was so agitated, he paced around the room, wringing his hands. "I called around. No one knows anything. No one has seen him since eleven o'clock last night."

"What about the jail? Maybe . . ."

"No, I checked that too. He's not there." He stopped pacing and looked Grampy in the eyes. "Mr. Dawson, I'm afraid he's been kidnapped."

"Kidnapped! Doc, that's serious stuff."

"It's happened before. They know Aaron's our leader and I fear they've . . . how do you say it? Put him on ice? They're going to pick us off, one by one. No one is safe now. I'm afraid we've lost the battle. Oh, this is dreadful, dreadful! And poor Aaron . . . such a fine man!"

The doctor collapsed into a chair and buried his face in his hands. "I don't know what to do! I just don't know what to do!"

"Grampy," I whispered, "that face I saw in the window . . ."

"Yes?"

"It looked like . . . Aaron."

Grampy stared at me for a long moment. Then he

hitched up his jeans and paced over to the window. For a long time no one said a word. Then Grampy murmured, "Doc, that little rat-faced man we met the other night at the cafe . . . did I hear Aaron say he was a locksmith?"

The doctor seemed in a daze. "I don't know who you're talking about."

"Played the violin. Beady little eyes and a long nose. Looks like a rat."

"Bernard Marks?"

"That's him. Is he a locksmith?"

Dr. Frankel heaved a sigh and glanced around the room. "Yes, he's a locksmith, but I don't understand . . ."

"I've got a little idea. We'll need Bernie Marks."

Before we left the office, Grampy asked if Aunt Mattie could be moved to the ranch. Dr. Frankel removed his gold-rimmed glasses and rubbed his tired eyes. "Ordinarily, I'd say no, but under the circumstances . . . I think you'd better leave town, all of you, and the sooner the better. This is dreadful, dreadful!"

Back at the house, Grampy rushed into Aunt Mattie's room with such gusto that it scared Mother. Maybe she had dozed off, and when he burst into the room, she gave out a little squeal. "Daddy! Do you have to make so much noise?"

He glanced at Aunt Mattie, then turned to Mother. "Things are happening, Sara Helen, and I don't know where they're heading. Aaron's missing."

Mother's eyes grew wide. "Missing!"

"That's right, maybe kidnapped by the local thugs.

Me and Riley have a little job to do. We'll need to borrow a dress and some face paint. While we're gone, you pack up and be ready to leave town. As soon as we can, we're taking Mattie to the ranch."

Mother laid her head on Grampy's shoulder. "Oh Daddy, I'm scared!"

Grampy nodded and gave her a pat.

Chapter Eighteen

As soon as darkness fell, Grampy and I left the house and started walking down the hill toward town. Up until that moment, I hadn't given much thought to what we were about to do, but now . . . .

"Grampy, do you ever . . . get scared?"

"Scared? You bet. When I asked your grandmother to marry me, I was scared to death. When your momma was born, I didn't know how I was going to feed another mouth. Every once in a while, when I climb on a bronc, I'm scared he'll kill me. I know a whole lot about being scared, son, but I know that you have to live with it and go on."

"Are you scared now?"

He gave me a grin. "If you could hear my heart beating, you'd think it was a whole drum section. In a word, yes. How 'bout you?"

"I'm scared."

"Can you handle it?"

"Yes sir, I'll handle it."

He put his arm around me. "You're a good boy. Your daddy would be mighty proud of you, and so am I."

"Thanks. What are we going to do with the dress?"

"You'll see."

The night life of Sparrow was in full swing when we reached downtown. The streets were lit up as bright as day and music from four or five establishments mingled in the soft night air. Just south of the ice-cream parlor, we saw a man and woman who were passed out drunk in an alley. She wore a flaming red wig and it had slipped down over her eyes.

We kept to the shadows and made our way to the ice-cream parlor, crossed the street, and waited on the shadow-side of a laundry.

A few minutes later, we saw a man coming down the boardwalk. He was short, well dressed in a blue suit and black fedora hat, and carried a walking stick.

Grampy studied him and whispered, "I believe that's our Dr. Frankel. But where's the locksmith?"

The doctor stopped in front of the ice-cream parlor, glanced around, and leaned on his stick. Grampy stepped out of the shadows and waved. Dr. Frankel glanced around and hurried across the street.

"I sure hope you brought your friend," said Grampy.

Dr. Frankel looked at us through the lenses of his little wire-rimmed glasses. His eyes were a pretty shade of blue, but also filled with concern. "We came by different routes. What is this about?"

Grampy patted the air with his right hand. "Wait 'til we're all here. If our locksmith don't show up, there won't be anything to talk about."

Two men passed down the street. They were laughing and talking about a poker game. Three men approached from the opposite direction. They were swaying on unsteady legs and holding each other up, and bellowing "Yankee Doodle Dandy" in a chorus of bad singing. They moved on down the street.

I could see that Grampy was getting nervous. So was Dr. Frankel, but every time I had seen him, he had seemed nervous.

Then we caught sight of someone approaching from the south. The way he moved reminded me of a mouse: five steps, stop; ten steps, stop; five steps, stop. When he passed under a light, we could see that he was a man of slight build, maybe a little taller than Dr. Frankel. He wore a vest over a white shirt and a black golfer's cap on his head.

Dr. Frankel took a deep breath. "It's Bernie. He's always late. At his own funeral, he'll be late."

Grampy stepped out of the shadows and whistled. Bernie glanced up and down the street, then came toward us in a fast walk. He shook Grampy's hand and nodded to me and Dr. Frankel.

"I came as fast as I could," he whispered. "There was a fight in the street and policemen were there. I had to make a detour."

Grampy said, "Well, I'm glad to hear that the officers of the law are busy tonight."

Mr. Marks flashed a bitter smirk. "The law? What a mockery."

Dr. Frankel said, "Why are we here, Mr. Dawson? This is most unusual."

Grampy told them that Aaron might be a prisoner in a room in The Oasis. "Bernie, if we can get you up on the second floor, can you pick your way into a locked room?"

Mr. Marks reached inside his vest and brought out a set of tools wrapped in cloth. "It's my business. How will I get to the room without being seen?"

"You'll see." Grampy turned to me. "Son, why don't you try on that dress." While Mr. Marks and Dr. Frankel gave me odd looks, I pulled the dress over my head. I could hardly believe that we were going to attempt this.

When Grampy had explained the plan, Dr. Frankel frowned and shook his head. "But I don't understand why I'm here."

Grampy gave him a grin. "You just hang around in the street and stay out of sight. If it appears that things are going the wrong direction, maybe you can create a . . . uh . . . disturbance."

"What do you mean?"

"Well, Doc, you were smart enough to make it

through medical school. I figure you'll come up with something. Light a fire. Take off your clothes and run around naked."

The solemn Dr. Frankel cleared his throat. "Those aren't my skills, but I'll do my best."

"Good enough."

By then, I was wearing the dress and had tied the sash at the waist. Grampy set Mother's hat on my head and painted my face with lipstick and rouge. He stepped back and studied me.

"What do you think, boys?"

Dr. Frankel shook his head. "Not very convincing, I'm afraid. He's wearing men's boots, and the hair . . . it's not right."

Grampy snapped his fingers. "Wait right here."

He trotted across the street to the alley where we had seen the drunken couple, and returned with a red wig and a pair of patent leather shoes. He removed the straw hat and plunked the wig down on my head.

"There. Now he looks just like the rest of 'em. Here, son, see if these shoes fit."

I stuffed my feet into the shoes, which were so small that I had to crumple up my toes. "They're too small. I don't think I can wear them."

"Wear 'em. They look mighty pretty."

"Grampy, I'm not sure I can walk!"

He heaved a sigh. "Son, our forefathers wore rags on their feet in the snow at Valley Forge. You can wear those shoes for thirty minutes." Grampy turned to the others. "What do you think now?"

They nodded, even the skeptical Dr. Frankel, who said, "As you say, he looks no worse than the others on the street. Maybe it will work."

Grampy took a deep breath. "Well, are we ready?"

Mr. Marks and Dr. Frankel exchanged glances, and Mr. Marks said, "This is very risky. If we get caught, it won't be pleasant."

"I agree," said Grampy, "so let's not get caught. Riley, I'll meet you back at Mattie's house. I'll play my fiddle long enough to hold the crowd. If I don't make it back, take care of your momma."

Dr. Frankel offered his hand. "You're a brave man, Mr. Dawson. I admire you."

Mr. Marks offered his hand. "And I too."

Grampy smiled. "Well, we won't argue about 'brave.'" He turned to me and gave me a hug. "Be careful, boy."

"You too, Grampy."

He waved his hand in the air and walked out into the street, swinging his fiddle case in his right hand. Fear closed around me as I watched him. I had a feeling that I would never see him again.

We waited and watched in the shadows. Grampy walked up to the front of The Oasis and looked up at a string of electric lights that was stretched across the street.

He sat down on the front steps and pulled his fiddle out of the case. As he went through his usual tuning ritual, several men stopped to watch. He said something to them and they laughed. Then he set his hat, crown-side down, on the boardwalk, threw one leg over the other knee, and started playing.

More people drifted out of the dance hall, some women but mostly men. They gathered around Grampy and watched. When he finished the first tune, the crowd clapped and cheered, and he went into another one. More people came out of the dance hall. After the third tune, a couple of men dropped money into the hat. By now, they were clapping in time with the music, then several men pulled their ladies away from the crowd and started dancing in the street.

Mr. Marks nudged me with his elbow. "I think it's time to go. Don't forget, young man, we are having a merry time. You must be an actor now."

"Yes sir. I'll do my best." My knees were shaking.

"Well, good-bye, Dr. Frankel. This is most unusual, isn't it?"

Dr. Frankel was serious to the end. He gave his head a shake and waved good-bye.

With our arms draped around each other, Mr. Marks and I staggered out into the street and lurched toward the crowd in front of The Oasis. I had no problem staggering. My feet were so balled up in those shoes, I could hardly walk.

When we reached the edge of the crowd, Mr. Marks whispered, "Laugh, young man. You look stricken. Be merry."

Since I had never been drunk before, I had to guess how to behave. I just acted like a complete fool, throwing my arms in the air, shrieking, squealing, laughing, stumbling, and hanging on to Mr. Marks for support. At one point, I felt the wig slipping over to the side of my head and had to give it a quick adjustment.

But I soon realized that my most ridiculous behavior seemed normal in this crowd, because everyone else was behaving in the same raucous manner. I blended right in and nobody gave me a second look. We started dancing. Since I didn't know how to dance, this was an interesting experience, but I soon realized that Mr. Marks was no ballerina himself. I kicked his shins and he kicked mine. He tromped on my feet and I tromped on his.

Then I tripped and fell into the street. At first Mr. Marks seemed alarmed and darted his eyes around the crowd. Then he offered his hand and yelled, "Miss Riley, you have all the grace of a cow!"

People around us laughed, and we started dancing again. We worked our way up the steps and onto the boardwalk. I caught Grampy's eye and he gave me a nod. Mr. Marks reached out and dropped a quarter into the hat.

Grampy kept right on playing but gave us a grin and said, "Thank you, my good man."

We had reached the front door and were about to slip inside, when a big man in greasy overalls came up and snatched me into his arms. He looked down at me with drunken eyes and said, "Let's dance, shurrplum. I don't have to be back at the rig 'til daylight."

His legs were so wobbly, he could hardly stand up, and within two minutes he had stomped my feet three times with his big work boots. I could see Mr. Marks on the edge of the crowd, watching me with worried eyes and giving me the sign to hurry up. At last I tore myself out of the big man's grip, but in the process, my wig ended up in his left hand.

He stared at the wig as though it were a dead animal. Then he looked at my head, his eyes wide and wooden. He handed me back my hair, and muttered, "Sorry, ma'am. I think I've had too mush chin."

He stumbled away, fell off the boardwalk, and landed in the street. No one even noticed.

I adjusted my wig and started toward the door, but ran into a big man in a bowler hat. I was about to apologize for being so clumsy, when I found myself looking into the face of . . .

Constable McGreggor.

Chapter Nineteen

THE CONSTABLE WAS standing right behind Grampy Dawson, tapping his toe in time with the music and munching his ever present peanuts. When I saw his face, I was so scared I couldn't breathe. I was sure he would recognize me, and we would all be exposed and thrown in jail . . . kidnapped . . . murdered . . . I was terrified.

But he didn't recognize me. Blowing peanut fumes into my face, he said, "He sure can play that fiddle, can't he?"

In a squeaky falsetto voice, I said, "Oh yes sir. Excuse me." And I hurried through the crowd to the door, where Bernie Marks was waiting, his face as pale as death.

We crept into The Oasis. The gaming tables were almost empty. One man sat alone, slumped forward in his chair with his face resting on the table. A man and a woman hung on to each other at the bar, laughing while the bartender picked his teeth and gazed off into space.

We found the stairway, immediately inside the door and to the left. Arm in arm, we staggered our way up the stairs, with Mr. Marks clinging to the bannister and doing his best to make jolly noise. At the landing, we dropped the charade and hurried up to the top. There, we came to a closed door. Mr. Marks turned the knob and found that it was unlocked.

We slipped through the door and found ourselves in a long empty hall, with doors on both sides. Mr. Marks whispered, "Which room?"

I had to think, and tried to imagine that I was out on the street, looking up at the window where I had seen the face. I pointed to a room on the south side of the hall, #204. We hurried over to it. Mr. Marks glanced up and down the hall, then brought out his tools. Most of them were small and resembled dentist's tools.

While I listened to the pounding of my heart, he selected a tool and slipped it into the lock.

Click, click, click.

He turned the doorknob and pushed. It didn't open. He selected another tool and slipped it into the lock.

Down on the street, Grampy was sawing away on his fiddle. He hardly even paused between tunes, and the sounds coming from the crowd indicated that he was making a big hit.

At last I heard a different sort of clicking sound. Mr. Marks had picked the lock and had opened the door a crack. He gave me a nod and we entered the room. He eased the door shut. The room was dark except for the light coming from the street.

I could see a bed, a dresser, a chair, and a night stand with a white porcelain pitcher sitting on top of it. We crept forward a few steps. The boards on the floor squeaked with every step. It seemed so loud, I was sure everyone in town would hear it.

Near the middle of the room, Mr. Marks stopped, and in a loud whisper he called, "Aaron? Aaron? It's Bernie Marks. Are you here?"

We heard the squeak of bed springs. A shadowy form sat up in the bed, then got to his feet. My scalp began to tingle. This didn't look right. Something was wrong. The man came toward us, weaving and dragging his feet. In the dim light, I caught a glimpse of his face: dark eyes, long sharp nose, hair sagging over his forehead, and pockmarks on his cheeks.

I had never seen him before.

Mr. Marks gave me a look of alarm, and I whispered, *"We're in the wrong room!"*

The stranger stared at us through squinted eyes. Then he spoke. "Tommy, is that you? It ain't time to go to work yet, is it? Seems like I just got to sleep."

Mr. Marks started backing out. "Sorry, friend. We got the wrong room. Go back to sleep."

The man yawned and muttered, "Don't you worry about that, buddy."

We backed out the door. Out in the hall, Mr. Marks stabbed me with a dark glare, but was nice enough not to scold me. I studied the doors again and pointed this time to #202. Mr. Marks lifted his brows to say, "Are you sure?" I nodded, and he went to work with his tools. This time he had the right tool and the job went fast. He motioned for me to wait in the hall. He crept inside and called, "Aaron? Aaron Kaplan?"

There was a long silence, then a voice said, "Yes! Over here."

I almost fainted with relief. I dived inside the room and eased the door shut. I could make out the silhouette of a man over by the window. He rose to his feet and I heard the clanking of chains. Bernie was already at work on Aaron's wrist manacles. *Click, click, click.* Then a chain hit the floor, and Aaron Kaplan was standing in front of me.

His eyes widened and he whispered, "Who are you?" I pulled off the wig and his face bloomed into a smile. "Riley! So you *did* see me!"

Aaron patted me on the shoulder and struck a match. He lit a kerosene lamp and turned up the wick. As the light spread across the room, I saw another man chained to the bed—a rough-looking man with long black hair. He grinned and waved a finger at me.

"Hello, kid. Small world, ain't it? I don't suppose

you've got any Prince Albert. I'm about to die for a smoke."

It was Charlie, the moonshiner!

I turned to Aaron. "I've met that man. He's a moonshiner."

"Oh? Well, he thinks he's also a Texas Ranger."

"A Texas Ranger! He was running a moonshine still in our canyon."

Aaron shrugged. "He said he was working undercover, and he's carrying a Ranger badge in his boot. It looked real to me."

Bernie picked the lock on Charlie's chains and he joined us. He wore a casual smile and didn't seem the least bit concerned about our situation. He patted me on the arm.

Aaron blew out the light and said, "Well, boys, let's see if we can get out of here."

In whispers, we discussed our plan for escape. I gave Aaron my dress and wig and he pulled them on, then smeared some lip paint on his mouth. It was so dark, he could hardly see himself in the mirror, and he painted a crooked mouth.

Aaron peered out into the hall, gave us the "all's clear" sign, and we slipped down the stairs. At the street door, Aaron spotted Constable McGreggor in the crowd and winced, but the constable's back was turned to us and he was listening to the music. Aaron slipped out first, followed by Charlie and Bernie.

Grampy played the last notes of his song and nodded at the applauding crowd. I was about to slip away when I saw Constable McGreggor tap Grampy on the shoulder. I froze and listened.

"Say, fiddle player, I just figured something out. Me and you have met before."

Grampy turned around, looked into the constable's face, and grimaced. "Oh?"

"It was in a canyon. You was playing that fiddle, as I recall, and . . . let's see, didn't you do some trick riding on a horse?" The constable laughed.

Grampy said, "Uh . . . my memory's a little hazy."

The constable cracked a peanut. "It's kind of a coincidence that we'd meet again, ain't it? What brings you to town?"

"My sister's not well."

The constable nodded. "That's right! Mrs. Sparrow. I hope she's feeling better."

"We've got her a good doctor."

The constable laughed. "This modern medicine's a wonderful thing. Well, keep playing. I sure love a fiddle."

Grampy cranked up another tune, and I disappeared into the crowd. I hated to leave Grampy all by himself, but I didn't know what else to do.

I ran all the way back to the house, and caught up with Aaron and Charlie as they were going inside. I went looking for Mother. I knew she'd be worried, and I found her in Aunt Mattie's room, sitting beside the bed. Aunt Mattie's eyes were open and she was talking.

"How long have I been like this, Sara Helen?"

"I'm not sure. Since Uncle George passed away. We got here a few days ago. We had no idea . . ."

Aunt Mattie raised her hand. "I know, sweetie. I couldn't talk or open my eyes, but I heard it all. I guess Ben Wallace has made me a pauper. I've been such a fool!"

Mother patted her hand. "Shhhh. Try to rest. We're going to take you away from here, just as soon as Daddy gets back."

Aunt Mattie gave a little laugh and closed her eyes. "Abner Dawson. I never thought I'd live to see the day . . ."

She drifted off to sleep, and Mother and I slipped out of the room. Out in the hall, she threw her arms around me and gave me a big hug. "Riley, I'm so glad you're back! How did it go?"

I pointed to Aaron. He had removed his disguise and was talking with Coy. For the first time, I noticed that Aaron's face was bruised and swollen, and one of his eyes had been blackened.

Mother went over to him. "Aaron, what did they do to you!"

He told us his story. After the meeting of the reform group, he was walking alone through town, on his way to Dr. Frankel's house, when two men jumped him from behind. After a struggle, they beat him to the ground, covered his head with a pillowcase, and dragged him to the room in The Oasis, where he was chained to the bed along with Charlie.

Mother said, "Who's Charlie?"

Aaron pointed to the man using the telephone. "Choctaw Charlie is what he called himself, and he seems to think he's an undercover agent for the Texas Rangers. I guess we'll find out."

Charlie hung up the phone and came over to us. He had tied his long greasy hair into a ponytail, but he still looked disreputable. "Well, it's all set. The Thirty-second Rangers are camped at a ranch five miles south of town. They're going to start this way."

Aaron said, "So you really are a Ranger? I was never sure."

We listened as Charlie told us about himself. His real name was Charles Mason. He had taken on the alias of Choctaw Charlie upon moving to Sparrow in the winter of 1926 to work undercover for the Rangers. After spending a few months hanging around town and running errands for a local bootlegger, he had been offered the job of running a new moonshine still in Hemphill County—the one on our ranch.

"Their plan," he told us, "was to make it the biggest still in the whole northern Panhandle. What you boys saw," he nodded to me and Coy, "was just the first stage. Over a period of six months, they planned to make it four times as big, with four or five men working it. As you probably figured out, your ranch was the perfect place for it: rough, isolated, almost impossible to reach, and far from anyone with a badge."

He turned to Mother. "And of course it was very convenient, since Ben Wallace had wormed his way into George Sparrow's business. He'd probably been planning to use the ranch for a year or more, and when

Mr. Sparrow died, he saw his big chance. The only problem was Mrs. Sparrow."

Mother nodded. "And he was slowly poisoning the life out of her."

Charlie nodded. "We've been gathering evidence against this mob for six months. All we needed was a call for help from the local citizens, and Aaron's group took care of that when they petitioned the governor."

When Charlie finished his story, we broke up into several groups and Charlie darted out on the porch to roll a smoke. I followed him outside.

"Mr. Mason, where did you go after we saw you that day in the canyon?"

Charlie laughed. "Well, kid, one of my partners in the gang . . . you met him. Remember Red? Red was a sly fox and he was selling whiskey on the side to a bootlegger. Constable McGreggor knew somebody was stealing, and he thought it was me. For some reason, they didn't kill me, but brought me to town and locked me up in their private jailhouse, The Oasis." He laughed again. "There I was, right in the middle of thieves and moonshiners. They never had any idea I was a Ranger, but they thought I was stealing their whiskey!"

I pulled the gold coin out of my pocket and handed it to Charlie. "I found a whole sack of these in the school stove. Do you suppose . . ."

Charlie took the coin and held it up to the light. "Well, I'll be! Yes sir, that would be Red's stash. He never trusted paper money." He handed me back the coin and gave me a wink. "You know, kid, if we can get to that gold before Red does, I'll see that you get your part of it. What do you think of that?"

I beamed a smile. "I think that would be wonderful, sir. I'd like to buy something nice for my mother."

Charlie patted me on the shoulder. "We'll see what we can do."

Just then, the telephone rang inside the house. Mother stuck her head out the door and said that the call was for Charles Mason.

Chapter Twenty

CHARLIE'S CONVERSATION ON the telephone didn't last long. When he hung up the receiver, he called everyone together and addressed the group.

"Folks, that was my captain. I have to go meet the Rangers at a rendezvous point south of town, so listen carefully. The Rangers will march into Sparrow around daylight. Their first objective will be to arrest and disarm every peace officer, and place the town under martial law." Aaron let out a cheer, but Charles Mason raised his hand for silence. "Don't celebrate just yet, Aaron. We've still got seven hours before that happens, and they're going to be dangerous hours for all of you." He turned to Mother. "Mrs. McDaniels, you folks need to load up and get out of town."

Mother nodded. "We're packed and ready, as soon as Daddy gets here."

"Good." Charlie's eyes went to Aaron. "When McGreggor learns that you've escaped, he'll tear the town apart looking for you. It could get very nasty. I'd advise you to leave town with Mrs. McDaniels's family."

Aaron smiled. "Good advice, but no thank you. I've been working toward this for a whole year. I want to be here when the Rangers march into town."

Charlie heaved a sigh and rolled his eyes up to the ceiling. "Aaron, you've done your part. Back off and let us finish the job. Lay low for twenty-four hours."

"No. I'll stay with the family until they get on the road. You go on about your business."

Charlie shrugged. "Well, you're on your own. This is McGreggor's town until we can slap a jailhouse around him. Watch your step."

"I've been watching my step for a long time, Charlie. It's second nature by now."

Aaron and Charlie shook hands. Charlie wished us well and went out into the night.

When the door closed, a heavy silence moved over us. Aaron snapped open his pocket watch and scowled at it. "It's almost midnight. Abner should have been back by now." He looked up and saw that Mother was watching him. He smiled. "What?"

"Mr. Mason was right. You're not safe in this dreadful place. Come with us to the ranch. Please?"

"Sara, this is all new to you. For me, it's just an-other . . ." Aaron cocked his ear and listened. We all heard the sound: someone outside was singing. Aaron brought a finger to his lips and crept to the front win-dow. He heaved a sigh of relief.

A moment later the door opened and Grampy walked in, carrying his fiddle case. He ran his eyes over us and said, "What are y'all doing up so late?"

Mother's head slumped down on her chest. "Daddy, where have you been! We've been worried sick about you."

"Well, sugar, once I'd started that deal, I couldn't just pick up and leave. Those people were having a ball and," he patted a bulge in his pocket, "I made fifteen dollars. Besides, my biggest fan happened to be the local constable, and I didn't figure he needed to be snooping around town." He hitched up his pants. "What's the plan?"

Aaron filled him in on everything that had hap-pened. "Now, Abner, we've got to get you folks on the road. When the police find . . ."

We all heard the sound of a car pulling up in front of the house. Mother's face turned pale and she pulled Coy close to her. Aaron rushed to the window. When he turned around, his eyes were grim. *They're here!* Aaron's dark eyes skipped around the room. "All you can do is try to bluff your way out of it. They're look-ing for me. I'll hide in the attic. You must be calm, all of you."

He ran up the stairs and climbed through a crawl

space into the attic. Grampy blinked his eyes and said, "Well, let's drift into Mattie's room and pretend we're ministering to the sick and the wounded."

We all moved into Aunt Mattie's room and took seats around her bed. Her face seemed to have gotten some color back, and I noticed that the covers on her bed had been disturbed. Her mouth was open slightly and I could hear her breathing, but otherwise she lay motionless.

We heard a loud knock at the front door. Grampy signaled Mrs. Kelly to answer it, but she didn't need to. The door burst open and we heard heavy footsteps on the floor, coming our way. A moment later, Constable McGreggor and Ben Wallace were standing in the door. Ben Wallace's face was tight and angry.

McGreggor wore a smirk. He nodded to Grampy. "Well, well, it's the fiddle player. Me and you keep running into each other."

Grampy nodded a greeting. "I get around."

"That was mighty pretty music and I think everyone had a nice time. But you know what? While you were playing, a couple of prisoners escaped from a room upstairs."

Ben Wallace narrowed his eyes at Grampy. "Where are they?"

Grampy put on an innocent face. "Hoss, you're asking me things I don't know anything about. I just got here, and the constable himself can vouch for where I've been."

Constable McGreggor had held his smile through

all of this, but now it turned cold. "Where's Kaplan? We know he's a pal of yours. He's a radical and a fugitive from the law. You'd best tell us and be quick about it."

Nobody moved or made a sound. All at once, an idea jumped into my head. I took a gulp of air and tried to hide the quiver in my voice. "Mister, if you'll let us go, I'll tell you who was stealing your whiskey."

All eyes swung around to me. Constable McGreggor had been chewing peanuts. His jaw froze in midchew. "What are you talking about?"

"It wasn't Choctaw Charlie."

McGreggor and Wallace traded looks. Then McGreggor said, "Go on."

"Will you promise to let us go?"

McGreggor said, "We'll think about it. Keep talking."

"Your thief was Red. He was selling to a bootlegger and he got his money in twenty-dollar gold picccs."

Wallace nodded. "All right. Where's the money?"

My heart was racing. "Let everyone go but me. When they're gone, I'll tell you."

The room fell silent. Wallace and the constable traded looks, and Wallace nodded his head. McGreggor pulled a big knife out of his pocket, opened the blade, and began cleaning his fingernails.

"You know, sonny, sharp steel can do terrible things to a face. And them scars never go away."

Mother let out a gasp. I didn't know what to do. I looked at Grampy. He raised one eyebrow and said, "Tell 'em, son. You've got no choice."

"All right. Red hid the money in the Notla school-house."

The constable's jaw dropped. Then he barked a dry laugh. "Ha! That country school out on the prairie? Why thunder, I was there just a week ago." The constable narrowed his eyes at me. "And you were there, weren't you? You were the brat with soot on his shirt."

"Yes sir. Red hid the money in the stove."

The constable put his knife back in his pocket. "Old Red, huh? I should have known. He's got pig eyes. That was a smart piece of work you did, sonny."

"Can we go now? Please?"

McGreggor cracked a peanut and popped the nuts into his mouth. "Where's Kaplan?"

Nobody spoke.

Before I knew what was happening, the constable grabbed me and put a choke hold on my neck. "Okay, fiddle player, start talking. Where's Kaplan?"

Just then, Aaron appeared at the door. "I'm here. Let him go."

McGreggor smiled and pushed me so hard that I almost fell down. He walked over to Aaron, jerked him into the room, spun him around, and frisked him.

Aaron said, "I don't carry weapons, McGreggor, you know that."

"When they find your body, you'll be carrying one. It'll improve the story in the morning paper." He twirled Aaron around. "How'd you get out of that room in The Oasis, huh?"

"I flew."

McGreggor slapped his face. "Was the fiddle player in on it? I'll bet he was. Who else? Talk, or I'll pull your tongue out with a pair of pliers."

Ben Wallace frowned. "That's enough, Joe. You'll have time for that later." He ran his eyes over our faces. "How's poor Mattie? Not so good, it seems. Alas. Well, you've gotten yourselves in a mess, and I really don't know what to do with you. How much do you know?"

Grampy said, "We know that Santy Claus comes on Christmas day and grapefruits grow on trees."

Wallace laughed. "Mr. Dawson, you're a funny man. I've really enjoyed getting acquainted with you but . . ." He gave his head a mournful shake. ". . . I'm afraid you know too much for your own good. You've figured out our little game, I guess. Haven't you?" Grampy said nothing. "I thought so. Well, Sparrow is a dangerous place. Every morning, the paper is full of stories of men who stayed out too late and went places they shouldn't have gone. And fiddle players, well, they're always keeping bad company."

He turned his eyes to Mother. "But what are we going to do with you, Mrs. McDaniels? You're such a pretty woman. And the boys, such handsome fellows. Did you know there's a market for pretty women? There is. And I hear there's a man in Dallas who buys children and uses them to pick cotton. That would be a sad life, I think."

Grampy studied the men. "Let 'em go, Wallace. You can have me and Aaron, but let my daughter and the boys go."

Mr. Wallace thought about that. "I'm afraid we've gone too far for that. Perhaps you've already figured out that Mattie Sparrow is going to pass away in a few days and leave me a substantial amount of property. I couldn't allow you to interfere with that. No, I'm afraid . . ."

Just then, an amazing thing happened. Aunt Mattie rose up from her bed, pulled a .45 Smith & Wesson revolver out from under the covers, and said, "Stand where you are, boys, or I'll shoot you dead. Abner, get their guns!"

Chapter Twenty-One

WE WERE ALL so shocked, no one could speak. Every eye went to the frail little woman in the blue and white nightgown. Her hair was pulled back in a tight bun and her face was pale, but there was fire in her blue eyes. She held the pistol with both hands, and it wasn't shaking.

Ben Wallace and the constable looked at each other, then lifted their hands in the air.

Aunt Mattie yelled, "Abner, for crying in the bucket, *get their guns!* I'd dearly love to shoot both of 'em, but I don't want to mess up the house."

Grampy and Aaron moved quickly and disarmed the men.

Constable McGreggor turned to Wallace and said, "Bennie Boy, I thought you'd taken care of the old hag."

"Shut up." Wallace turned a smile to Mattie. "Mattie, put it down. You don't know what you're doing. You've been sick. I'm your friend."

"Sure you are," she said, watching him down the barrel of the pistol. "With friends like you, I could have been buzzard bait. I ought to shoot you, Ben Wallace. You're a cheat, a liar, and a low-life coward. George tried to warn me about you, but I didn't listen."

"Mattie, Mattie, you've got this all wrong. Put down the gun and . . ." He took a step toward her.

"Stand your ground, Ben, or I'll rid the world of a rat! Abner, are you just going to stand there? Find some rope and tie 'em up!"

Grampy and Aaron hurried out of the room. Ben Wallace spoke in a soft voice. "Mattie, listen to reason. What you're doing is very serious. Constable McGreggor is an officer of the law. You'll be charged with a felony, and I'll have to testify against you. We don't want that. They'll take you to jail, Mattie. Jail. Think about it. Be reasonable."

"By netties," she said, "let 'em charge and let 'em prosecute. They can't eat me." Grampy and Aaron had returned by then with some drapery cord. Aunt Mattie yelled, "Tie 'em up, boys, tie 'em up tight!"

Grampy and Aaron tied up the crooks, with their hands behind their backs, and pushed them down in chairs. Constable McGreggor wore a sneer throughout and kept his eyes on Aunt Mattie. "You won't get by with this, you old witch. My men know we came here. You'll never get out of town, and I'll personally see that you spend the rest of your life in the pen."

"We'll see about that, I reckon." Aunt Mattie lowered the pistol and handed it to Grampy. "Here, take this thing. I'm as weak as a pup." She sank back into her pillows, then cut her eyes at Grampy. "Abner, I was in this bed nearly a month before you came to check on me. And I noticed that you skipped George's funeral."

"Mattie, I was up in Kansas."

"Playing that blasted fiddle, I'll wager." She turned to Mother. "I always told him that fiddle was going to be the ruin of him." She turned back to Grampy. "Abner, hell's so full of fiddle players, their arms and legs are sticking out the windows. You should have been here two weeks ago!"

"Mattie, I think I liked you better when you were sick."

Aaron stepped in. "Maybe you two could finish this later. You need to leave. Now."

The constable was leaning back in his chair, still wearing his smirk. "Kaplan, we ain't done with you."

Aaron gave him a smile. "We'll see about that, I suppose." Aaron turned to Grampy. "Let's go."

Grampy nodded. "Boys, y'all get the bags, and don't forget my fiddle. Aaron, help me carry this nagging old woman out to the truck."

Mattie slid her legs over the side of the bed and stood up. "Nobody needs to carry me anywhere. I'll walk on my own two legs." She took a step and sank. Aaron caught her before she hit the floor. She looked into his face. "You're the nice man who runs the clothing store, aren't you? Do you reckon you could help me out to the truck?"

Aaron picked her up in his arms. Grampy smirked and said, "Mattie, you'll be real disappointed to know that he plays the fiddle."

She looked into Aaron's face. "Is that true?"

"No, Mrs. Sparrow. The violin."

Mattie shot Grampy a triumphant look. "I knew it! He plays the *violin*, Abner. He looks too wholesome to be a fiddle player."

Grampy started to say something, but just then the telephone rang. We all traded puzzled looks, then Grampy motioned for me to answer it. While the others went out to the truck, I ran into the hall and picked up the phone.

It was Dr. Frankel. "Riley? Tell Aaron that some policemen are trying to burn his store! Oh, this is dreadful . . ." The line went dead.

I hung up the phone and ran out to the truck.

Grampy and Aaron had just placed Aunt Mattie in the passenger's seat, and Mother wrapped her in blankets. I blurted out the news.

Aaron stared at me with uncomprehending eyes. "What?"

"That was Dr. Frankel on the phone. Some of the

constable's men are trying to burn down your store."

Aaron's hand went up to his brow. "How can they do this?" Then, suddenly, he stood straight up. "My books!" He turned to Grampy and Mother. "Goodbye and God be with you."

Mother stepped over to him and seized his arm. "Aaron, no! Please stop and think. It might be a trap."

Aaron's dark eyes had lost their focus and he seemed to be talking to himself. "I won't let them do this!"

"Aaron, Aaron, listen to reason!" Mother cried. "The books can be replaced, but you can't be."

Calm returned to Aaron's face. He smiled at Mother and patted her hand, then gently removed it from his arm. "I'll do what I must do. Abner, drive as fast as you can and don't stop for anything. Leave now. Good-bye."

He gave each of us a nod, then turned and started off toward town. Mother called after him, "Aaron, the map! The map!" There was no reply. Mother shook her head and whispered, "They knew how to draw him out, didn't they?"

Grampy nodded. "I'm afraid so, honey. Well, we need to get Mattie out of town. I'm sure they don't want her on the witness stand. Riley, crank this thing and let's get on the road."

I gave it a crank. The motor coughed a few times, then started. Grampy adjusted the spark lever until the motor leveled off to a steady roar. Mother, Coy, and I climbed into the back end and settled ourselves on the bedrolls, and we lurched away. Mrs. Kelly stood at the gate, and we waved good-bye.

Coy nestled into Mother's arms and started crying. "Mother, I'm scared. They won't do anything bad to Aaron, will they?"

"We'll hope for the best. Aaron's a very smart and resourceful man. We'll all say a prayer for him, won't we?"

Ten minutes later we made it over the big hill east of Marshall Creek. Below us, and spread out in all directions, were the lights of town, oil derricks, oil processing plants, and the headlights of cars moving through the darkness. And the orange glow of a fire near the center of town.

We coasted down the other side of the hill and the lights disappeared, leaving us in pitch blackness except for the headlights of the truck. The cool night air moved around us and I felt Mother shiver.

"Daddy, give me the pistol." She reached through the back window of the cab and took the pistol. She handed it to me. "You're the man of the house now, Riley. If we're followed, use it."

I took the pistol and swallowed a lump in my throat.

For the first hour, Mother, Coy, and I sat in the back of the truck with our eyes locked on the road behind us, dreading the moment when we might see a pair of headlights in the distance. But it appeared that luck was on our side. We sped through the night and had the road all to ourselves. The rest of the world was asleep, it seemed, and as we moved farther and farther away from Sparrow, we dared to relax a little bit.

A big yellow moon had come up in the east, and it gave enough light so that I could see Coy's face. It was innocent, owlish, and frightened. I noticed that Mother was looking at me, an odd little smile on her mouth. I asked her what she was thinking.

"You didn't tell me a word about that sack of gold. Are we keeping secrets from each other now?"

"I thought you might worry."

"Riley, I don't want you going back to the school. Promise me you won't."

"All right, Mother, I promise." And in my mind, I added, ". . . that I'll get there before Red does." That's what Tom Sawyer would have done.

The hours crept by. At Pampa, Grampy turned left onto the two-rut trail that would take us thirty miles north to the Canadian River.

Mother called out, "Daddy, are you still awake?"

"Oh yeah, doing fine. I just saw thirteen purple billy goats standing in the road, but I missed 'em."

"Daddy, don't make jokes. If you get sleepy, stop and walk around."

"All right, sugar. Anybody on our tail?"

"It's all clear."

"Good. Maybe those hammerheads found some-body else to chase around."

In a soft voice, Mother said, "Daddy has surprised me. All those years when I was growing up, he seemed as irresponsible as a grasshopper, but he's really shown

175

some grit this past week. Some men take longer to ripen than . . ."

"*Mother, there's a car behind us!*"

I had seen a brief flash of light, maybe four or five miles to the south, then it disappeared behind a hill. But as we peered into the night, we saw it again.

Mother leaned up to the window. "Daddy, somebody's behind us. Maybe you'd better speed up."

The road was rough enough so that he should have slowed down, not sped up, but he gave the truck more gas and soon we were feeling the ruts and potholes in the road. Coy woke up and looked around.

"What's wrong?" I pointed to the headlights. "Oh my gosh!"

It wasn't long before all the jolting brought Aunt Mattie out of her sleep. "Abner, slow this thing down before you break our necks!"

"Mattie, there's somebody following us."

"Well . . . try to miss some of the holes in this road. Just because they're there don't mean you have to hit 'em."

"I'm doing my best, Mattie."

"Well . . . we never know about you. You've pulled so many mean tricks on me, I never know what to expect."

Mother called out, "Daddy, they're gaining on us! Can you go any faster?"

"Put a gag in this woman's mouth and I'll see what I can do."

He gave the truck more gas, and now we really

were having to hang on to keep from being thrown out. After one particularly violent jolt, one of the headlights went dead. If we lost the other light, we would be driving in the dark.

Mother and Coy and I kept our eyes locked on the lights behind us. It was clear now that they were getting closer. Whoever that was, they were driving even faster than we were.

We sped down the long hill that led to Chicken Creek. Grampy didn't slow down at all, and hit the creek crossing with a full head of steam. Water flew in all directions, and up in the front, Aunt Mattie let out a squeal.

We started up the last hill between us and the river. The road had turned to pure sand. We could hear the tires slipping.

"Daddy, hurry, hurry! They're getting closer!"

My heart was pounding and I could feel sweat in the palms of my hands. I reached down and took a grip on the pistol.

Chapter Twenty-Two

WE PLOWED OUR way up the sandy hill and started down the other side. Grampy yelled, "There's the river, and I can see a light in Old Man Lehman's house!"

It was then that I realized that we had been driving for four hours, and the first light of dawn was showing on the eastern horizon. Mr. Lehman was already up and doing his chores.

Grampy yelled out, "I'll drive to the riverbank and y'all be ready to run. Forget the bags. Mattie, wake up, you're fixing to get wet! We've got to wade the river."

We drove to the edge of the water, and there we

came to a sudden stop. Grampy killed the motor and we all scrambled out of the truck. The car was bearing down on us. The headlights cast eerie shadows on the saltgrass and brush.

Grampy yelled, "Who's got the pistol? Give it to me." I handed him the pistol. "Son, you're going to have to help Mattie across. Sara Helen, grab Coy and run! Head for the house and don't stop for anything!"

I dragged Aunt Mattie from the cab, threw her arm around my neck, and started for the river. "Grampy, come on!" He was standing beside the truck, holding the pistol up at shoulder level and watching the approaching lights. We could hear the drone of the motor now.

He gave me a smile. "Go on, son. Maybe I'll see you when the smoke clears."

I waded out into the river and didn't look back.

Aunt Mattie was too weak to get much use out of her legs and I had to drag her through the water. It was a good thing that she didn't weigh any more than she did, and that the river had gone down since we'd crossed it before. The water was only shin-deep.

I waded out to dry land and turned to get one last look at Grampy. The car slid to a stop. Grampy crouched behind the truck and drew down with the pistol.

There was a moment of dead silence, then we heard a man's voice. "Abner, don't shoot! It's me, Abe Frankel! I've got Aaron. He's been hurt."

By then, I could see Aaron's blue Chevrolet, "the fastest car on the road." They had followed us, using Mother's map.

Grampy slumped down on the truck bed and lowered the pistol. Then his voice drifted across the river. "Doc, you don't know how close you came to getting shot!"

I left Mother and the others, and waded back across the river. I could hear Dr. Frankel talking in an agitated voice. "Wallace and McGreggor got loose. We passed them on our way out of town."

Grampy said, "Did they follow you?"

"I don't know. Aaron has a broken arm. I need to set it as soon as possible."

Grampy's eyes darted back and forth as he tried to come up with a plan. "Doc, Aaron's going to have to suffer for a while longer. We've got to push on to the ranch. Riley, how deep is the river?"

"Maybe a foot deep."

"Good. We don't have time to wait for Rudolph's team. Let's see if we can drive across."

Luck was with us. The river bottom was firm and hadn't filled in with quicksand. Grampy drove the truck across and Dr. Frankel followed in the car. On the north bank, Grampy called for Mother and Aunt Mattie to join us, then we started our last leg of the journey home.

I rode in the car with Dr. Frankel. He sat stiff and straight in the seat, gripping the wheel with both hands. For a long time, hours it seemed, he didn't say a word, but when I asked him what had happened to Aaron, he told me the story.

After leaving Aunt Mattie's house, Aaron made his way through town to his store. Someone had started a kerosene fire on the front door and boardwalk, and Aaron and several men tried to put it out. But then a policeman recognized Aaron and attacked him with a billy club. Aaron blocked the blow with his left arm, which broke the arm, but then he proceeded to knock the policeman unconscious with a blow to the chin.

I was amazed. "Aaron did that?"

Dr. Frankel sniffed. "Aaron's not as meek as he appears. He was a champion boxer at his high school in Illinois." He gave me a sideward glance. "I hope your mother doesn't mind us intruding like this, but I felt Aaron's life was in danger."

"We're all glad you came. But what about Aaron's store?"

Dr. Frankel shook his head and kept driving.

It took us two hours to make the twenty-mile drive to our ranch. Turk heard us coming and ran out to give us an escort. Spud came out of the barn and waved.

Grampy and I helped Aaron out of the car and up to the house. His face was ashen and he was gritting his teeth against the pain. Grampy told Spud to sit on the porch and watch the road for any approaching vehicles.

We laid Aaron on the kitchen table and Dr. Frankel removed his jacket and rolled up his shirt sleeves. He told Mother to find material for a splint and a sling, then said that Coy and I should wait out-side.

"I think Aaron would prefer it that way."

Coy and I walked down to the barn. Coy said, "Why'd we have to leave?"

"Because the doctor's going to set Aaron's arm. It's painful, and I guess Aaron doesn't want an audience. Would you?"

Coy thought about it for a minute. "I suppose not."

When the horses saw us coming their way, they threw up their tails and raced into the corrals. I guess they thought they could coax some feed out of us. They usually did. All at once it occurred to me . . .

. . . that I had a horse in the corral . . .

. . . and that all the adults were occupied inside the house.

I looked down at my brother. "Coy, can you keep a secret? And I'm not talking about a little secret. A seri-ous secret?"

He gave me a puzzled look. "I guess so. What?"

"Swear on the Bible? Cross your heart and hope to die?" He nodded. "I'm going to ride up to the school."

His eyes widened. "The gold? Riley, mother told you . . ."

"Shhh. If I'm not back in two hours, send Grampy and Spud. Can I trust you?"

He pressed his lips together. "All right, I'll do it. But you have to promise that you'll never call me 'O Little One' again."

"You're a hard man, Coy, but I think we can do business."

We sealed the deal with a handshake. Ten minutes later, my mare and I slipped away from headquarters and headed north.

Chapter Twenty-Three

THREE HUNDRED YARDS west of the schoolhouse, I stopped and studied the situation ahead.

The only sound came from the wind sighing in the cedar trees around the school, and the groan of a few passing cars on the road just north of the school. It was one of the main east-west arteries in the Texas Panhandle, a dirt road that had been widened and improved with gravel.

As far as I could see, the school was deserted, with no sign that anyone had been there in the last week. But then I noticed the ears of my mare. They stood straight up and she was looking at something. This caused a tingle of fear to scamper down my back, but then I saw what had gotten Dolly's attention: a skunk was ambling along nearby, looking for bugs.

I patted Dolly on the neck and nudged her with my heels, and we rode up to the schoolhouse. I climbed out of the saddle and tied her to a cedar tree. I checked the ground for tracks, just to be certain Red wasn't around. I didn't see any tracks.

I looked over both shoulders and started up the steps, turned the knob and pushed open the door. I peeked inside. The school was empty and quiet.

I closed the door and tiptoed over to the stove. I don't know why I tiptoed, but it just seemed the right thing to do. I bent down, opened the door, and peered inside.

The stove was empty!

My heart sank. Red had beat me to the money, maybe by only a matter of hours or minutes. If we'd only . . .

Suddenly I heard something behind me. I turned my head slowly around . . . and found myself looking straight into the green eyes of *Red himself!*

I gasped for breath and jumped back. Red had a shotgun resting on his shoulder, and he didn't appear to be in a jolly mood.

"How'd you know about my money, and where's it at?"

I swallowed hard and stammered a reply. "I found it when I was cleaning the stove, but I didn't take it. I just got here."

Red wiped his mouth with the back of his hand, but never took his eyes off me. "I know you just got here, 'cause I rode in right behind you. I follered you for half a mile. You ain't much of a frontiersman, to be a ranch kid." Red's eyes darted around the room. "McGreggor done it. Had to be him, the cheating scum, but I don't know how he knew about it."

At that very moment, the two doors on Miss Cates's supply closet burst open and out stepped two men, both armed with short-barreled shotguns. Red was as shocked as I was. He whirled around but had enough good sense not to provoke a fight, since the two men had him covered.

The taller of the two men flashed a smile full of pearly teeth and said, "Small world, huh kid?"

I stared at him in disbelief. *It was Choctaw Charlie!*

He motioned for Red to lay down his shotgun. "Sit down, Red. I wouldn't want you to try anything foolish." Red squeezed his fat behind into one of the desks. Charlie lowered his shotgun, while the other man kept Red covered. "Red, would it surprise you to know that I was working undercover for the Texas Rangers?"

Red's jaw dropped. "Naw! You weren't . . . were you?"

Charlie opened his vest and showed the badge on his shirt. "Sparrow's finished, Red. The Rangers moved in this morning at daylight."

Red's head sank. "Maybe you could let me go, Charlie. We was friends. I've got a wife and two kids over in Oklahoma."

"Well, she's a lucky woman, Red, 'cause she'll be

rid of you for several years. Sorry, you broke the law." Charlie turned to the other Ranger. "Johnny, put the cuffs on him and watch him. Me and this boy have business to discuss."

Charlie motioned for me to follow him outside. He must have noticed that I was burning up with curiosity. "You look kind of surprised, kid."

"Every time I've seen you I've been surprised."

He chuckled. "Well, the Rangers rolled into town around five o'clock. They disarmed all the local thugs and not a shot was fired. Everything seemed to be pretty well under control, so I thought I'd drift over here and check things out. You know, money draws crooks just like ants to sugar. Sure enough, old Red came to it."

"Did they catch Wallace and the constable?"

Charlie gazed out at the prairie and rolled a Prince Albert cigarette. "Not while I was there, but they won't get far."

"Did Aaron's store burn down?"

"Nope. It got some damage to the front, but that's all. I know, because I put out the fire." He struck a match with his thumbnail and lit his smoke. "Listen, kid, I've got a job for you. We left our car at that farmhouse over yonder. Some nice folks named Higgins dropped us off, so Red wouldn't know we were here. Reckon you could ride over there and ask Mr. Higgins to come pick us up?"

I tried not to show my excitement. That was Laura's house!

Charlie patted me on the shoulder. "I appreciate this. You'll get your reward."

I jumped on Dolly and headed west in a lope. I felt good enough to let out a yell, but with so many people walking around with shotguns, I decided maybe I'd better not.

I was the toughest, bravest kid on the Canadian River, and maybe even the richest. All the kids in the neighborhood would swoon when they read the papers: "Local Ranch Youth Cleans Out Gangsters and Becomes Wealthy." Jackie Tinsley would *bow* the next time he saw me, and Coy would be so awestruck that he would volunteer to do my dishes for the rest of our lives, even when we were old men.

The Higgins family lived in a neat white clapboard house that appeared to have been added on to several times, as more children came into the family and as the price of wheat allowed. Laura was sitting in the shade of the porch when I arrived. She and her sister were seated in the glider swing, and Laura was brushing Sally's hair, which was long, red, and frizzy like Laura's.

I tied my mare to an elm tree, waved a greeting, and then proceeded to jump the white picket fence. Laura's little sister noticed and was impressed. I think Laura was too, but she didn't always gush when she was supposed to.

I marched up to the porch and rested my right foot on the step. "Morning, ladies."

Laura looked at me with a puzzled smile. "Riley

McDaniels, what in the world are you doing over here?"

"Oh, just returning from my latest crusade, Miss Laura. I've cleaned the outlaws out of Sparrow, saved several damsels from terrible villains, and found the gold, and I confess, it's made me a little tired and thirsty."

She pushed the swing with her foot and gazed off at the sky. "Riley, what are you doing over here? When you're ready to tell me the truth, I'll listen."

"It'll have to wait, Laura. I need to speak to your father."

We left the porch and went looking for her father. We found Mr. Higgins on the south side of his shop, nailing iron shoes on a big workhorse. He wore his usual clothes: blue cotton shirt, brown pants held up with suspenders, and a straw hat whose shape described him as something more than a farmer but something less than a cowboy.

When he heard us rounding the corner of the shop, he looked and swatted a fly. We exchanged greetings and I told him that the Rangers needed their car.

"All right," he said, "you ride back to the school, and I'll come along directly. Laura, you might as well ride with him. Ruthie's in the corral."

Laura gave me a questioning look. I said, "I'd be honored, ma'am."

Ten minutes later, we set out on the three-mile ride across the flats to the school. Laura gave me a patient look and said, "All right, now tell me what you've been up to. And as Coy would say, 'No corn, please.'"

"Coy would never say please."

"Hurry up, Riley. Sometimes you're so annoying. Did you go to Sparrow? Did your mother go with you?"

"Yes, I went to Sparrow, and yes, Mother went with us. But Laura, you won't believe all the things that happened on that trip!"

We slowed our horses to a walk and I launched into all my stories. Now and then I shot a glance at Laura. She was listening to every word. When I came to the part about sneaking into The Oasis to save Aaron and Choctaw Charlie, she said, "Riley, weren't you just terrified?"

"I won't deny it. I was pretty scared." Off to the north, a car drove past, heading toward the school. "There goes your daddy. Yes, I was scared, Laura, but once we got into the room . . ."

"Riley?"

"Once we got into the room, it wasn't so . . ."

"Riley!" We were riding close enough to each other so that she could reach out and touch me, and I felt her hand on my left arm. "That wasn't the Rangers' car, and the man sitting on the right . . . Riley, I've seen him before. At the school. I think it was . . . *Constable McGreggor.*"

A shiver passed through my body at the mention of that name.

Chapter Twenty-Four

MY MOUTH WAS suddenly dry. "Laura, they know about the gold. If they stop at the school . . . we'd better get over there . . . fast!"

"Riley, they're turning in at the school!"

We spurred our mares into a full gallop and gave them their heads. We flew over the prairie, steering the mares around holes and clumps of Spanish dagger. Dolly and Ruthie were about evenly matched in a wide open race, and I could see Laura's red hair streaming out behind her and her dress flying around in the wind.

Up ahead, I could barely make out the shapes of two men. They got out of the car and went into the school. Minutes passed, and no one came out. Someone had pulled a gun on someone, but there was no way of knowing which way it had gone. Either the Rangers had captured the outlaws, or the outlaws had captured the Rangers.

Laura pointed to a car on the road to our left. "Riley, it's Daddy!" She waved her arms. Mr. Higgins waved back and kept driving. He must have thought we were racing our horses and playing around. "If he walks into the school . . ."

We galloped to the east. Mr. Higgins parked in front of the school and went inside. We waited and watched. He didn't come out again. I could see fear in Laura's eyes.

We stopped our horses fifty yards from the school. We had no weapons. The nearest telephone was ten miles away. There was nothing we could do.

Then I saw the skunk.

Maybe there *was* something we could do.

I took a deep breath and tried to hide the tremor in my voice and hands. "Laura, I'm going to try something, and it's pretty crazy." I told her my plan. "If anything goes wrong, ride for the canyons and hide."

She nodded. "Riley, are you shivering?"

I realized that my teeth were chattering. "I guess I'm a little nervous. Good-bye. I'll see you after the smoke clears."

I figured Grampy wouldn't have minded me borrowing one of his lines. I'd done it plenty of times before.

I left Laura with the mares. The skunk was digging in some soft dirt beneath a dried cow chip. He didn't seem to notice me. I tried to remember Spud's technique for snatching a skunk. This was no time to make a mistake.

When I had rehearsed it in my mind, I took a deep breath of air and started trotting toward the skunk. If he heard me coming and got scared, he would spray me with a stream of that horrible yellow stuff, and that would be the end of it. At close range, skunk musk was so powerful that it caused temporary blindness, and a direct hit in the eyes could cause permanent damage.

This was a gentle skunk and he was used to kids running and playing around the school. Maybe he wouldn't mind . . . I hoped that he was as gentle as he seemed.

Ten feet. Eight feet. Five feet. The skunk heard me and lifted his head. I ran up to him and snatched him by the tail. He clawed the air with his front paws and tried to reach up and bite me. I shook him back down and headed straight for the school, going over my plan as I ran.

I jumped the three steps and landed on the porch with a loud thud. The two Rangers, Laura's daddy, and Red were standing in front of the teacher's desk with their hands in the air. Wallace and McGreggor stood facing them, with their backs to me. They were holding guns.

When they heard me crash into the door, they whirled around, pointing their guns at me. I drew back my arm and heaved the skunk with all my might.

And then everything went crazy. I saw the look of total shock on the face of Ben Wallace as the skunk came flying at him. He lifted his hands to keep the skunk from hitting him in the face, but the skunk went off anyway, covering him and McGreggor with the stench of ten thousand onions, boiled in the fires of hell.

Suddenly they were coughing and screaming, gasping for air, gagging, staggering around and rubbing their eyes. Ranger Charles Mason gave me a startled look. Then, in a flash, he disarmed the crooks, handcuffed them, and ran outside for fresh air.

Gasping for breath, he said, "Kid, have you ever thought of joining the Rangers?"

When Wallace and McGreggor came stumbling out of the school, McGreggor glared at me through his stinging eyes and snarled, "I should have finished you off when I had the chance, you little brat."

"Yes sir, but you didn't. And you got beaten by a skunk."

Laura came running up to me, her eyes shining in wonder. "Riley McDaniels, how did you think of that? A skunk!"

"Are you impressed?"

She cocked her head to the side and gave me a cute little smile. "I am, I really am."

Wow! That made it all worthwhile. I had finally done something to impress Laura Higgins.

And suddenly it was all over. Our ordeal with the moonshiners had finally come to an end.

Well, almost.

Chapter Twenty-Five

THE NEXT MORNING at eleven o'clock, we held a little ceremony on the rim of Point Creek Canyon. Coy and Mother and Grampy were there, and Aaron with his arm in a sling; Dr. Frankel and Aunt Mattie Sparrow and Ranger Charles Mason. Oh, and Laura Higgins too. I had . . . that is, Mother had insisted we drive over to the Higgins place and pick her up.

We parked the cars just west of the canyon rim and walked over to the edge. It was a bright clear morning, with a gentle breeze rustling the wildflowers on the prairie. Ranger Charles Mason had come up with the idea and he presided over the ceremony.

Charlie was rolling a smoke as he talked. "Well, folks, yesterday the Rangers gave Sparrow back to its citizens. Today, we'll rid your ranch of a moonshine still." He struck a match with his thumbnail, lit his smoke, and pulled a bundle of something out of the pocket of his jacket.

It was three sticks of dynamite tied together.

He held it up so everyone could see, then turned to me. "I guess you're the one who ought to do the honors, kid."

"No sir, let Grampy do it. It was his fiddle that made it happen."

Charlie nodded. "Fair enough. Mr. Dawson?" Grampy gave me a nod of appreciation and took the bundle. "Throw it into that stand of cedars, and don't hold it too long. You'll have about thirty seconds, and then it's going to make a pop."

Grampy nodded and Charlie held his cigarette to the fuse.

The fuse caught fire and began to hiss. As calmly as you please, Grampy held out the dynamite to Aunt Mattie and said, "Here, Mattie, why don't you hold this?"

Aunt Mattie's eyes almost bugged out of her head, and she let out a screech—just what Grampy had hoped for. He cackled, walked over to the canyon rim, and lobbed the bundle into the canyon, placing it right in the middle of the cedar grove.

We covered our ears and watched. Moments later, the ground shook with a loud BOOM, and pieces of pipe, copper tubing, and oak barrels flew in all directions and filled the air.

Everyone clapped and cheered. Mother was beaming, and she proceeded to hug the neck of everyone present, even the solemn Dr. Frankel. When she came to Grampy Dawson, she wrapped her arms around his neck, kissed him on the cheek, and said, "Thank you, Daddy, thank you so very much!"

Aunt Mattie watched with narrowed eyes. "Well, Abner Dawson, you're a slow starter, but I have to admit that you finished pretty strong this time. But I still say that you'd be better off to throw that fiddle into the river."

Mother's gaze went from Grampy to Aunt Mattie. Then she smiled and said, "Oh, I think it'll be all right."

Arm in arm, hand in hand, we walked through the yellow wildflowers and drove back home, leaving a cloud of smoke hanging over Point Creek Canyon to mark the place where moonshiners had once inhabited our ranch.

Aaron and Dr. Frankel stayed with us for two days, then drove back to Sparrow. We hated to say good-bye to Aaron, but Coy and I had a feeling that we would be seeing more of him in the future.

On June 14, 1927, Sparrow held its first election after the lifting of martial law. Aaron Kaplan was elected mayor by a landslide.

On that same day, I received a check in the mail for $2,500, signed by the governor of Texas. It was my reward for helping the Rangers recover the moon-shiner's gold. I gazed at the check for a minute, then rushed over to Mother and handed it to her.

"This is for you, the bravest, finest mother in the whole world." Mother's eyes misted over and she pulled me into a hug. "And Mother, let's use it to make a down payment on the ranch. I think Daddy would be proud of us."

She nodded and brushed a tear from her eye. "Yes, I think he would."

John R. Erickson is the author of the popular Hank the Cowdog series, described by *USA Today* as "the best family entertainment in years."

Erickson lives on his own 8,500-acre ranch, which straddles the majestic Canadian River canyon in the Texas Panhandle. Eleven miles from the nearest paved road, he leads a cowboy's life riding the range on horseback, mending fences, and tending to his herd of cows, calves, and Black Angus bulls. But before the ranch work starts, John rises at 5:30 A.M. to write. The idea for *Moonshiner's Gold* began to form when he and his son Mark discovered the remains of seven moonshine stills on their property, which they believe operated during Prohibition.

The author of more than forty books for young readers, Erickson lives with his wife, Kris, near his boyhood home of Perryton, Texas.